VILLAGE OF FEAR

After narrowly escaping death on a train, two people find themselves in an eerie deserted village — and make a grisly discovery ... On a dark and stormy night, locals gather in an inn to tell a frightening tale ... A writer's country holiday gets off to a bad start when he finds a corpse in his cottage ... And a death under the dryer at a fashionable hairdressing salon leads to several beneficiaries of the late lady's will falling under suspicion of murder ...

NOEL LEE

VILLAGE
OF FEAR
& Other Stories

Complete and Unabridged

LINFORD
Leicester

First published in Great Britain

First Linford Edition
published 2019

Copyright © 2018 by Jan Layton-Smith

A catalogue record for this book is available
from the British Library.

ISBN 978–1–4448–4203–6

Published by
F. A. Thorpe (Publishing)
Anstey, Leicestershire

Set by Words & Graphics Ltd.
Anstey, Leicestershire
Printed and bound in Great Britain by
T. J. International Ltd., Padstow, Cornwall

This book is printed on acid-free paper

VILLAGE OF FEAR

1

The Beginning of it All

The girl didn't just enter the compartment: she fell into it. Michael caught her deftly as she stumbled across his feet, and as the train gathered speed out of the tiny station and an angry porter slammed the swinging door with a violence that shook the very windows, he set her down in the seat opposite. Then looking across at her, he said gravely:

'You know, that was really very silly. You might have hurt yourself.'

She was young and lovely and breathless.

'Ooh . . . Thanks a lot!' she gasped. 'Yes, I suppose it was. But you see, I had to — I simply had to — '

She stopped to regain her breath. She had soft hazel eyes and a little snub nose, and a ridiculous red hat that did nothing save emphasize the most glorious mass of golden-brown hair he had ever seen. Michael looked at her critically and felt that he ought to be annoyed with her . . . only you can't be annoyed with someone who is looking pale and frightened and thoroughly shaken-up. You can only be mildly disapproving.

'I should have thought it would have been better to have missed the train altogether rather than have risked breaking your neck like that,' he opined; but he found that she was not even listening. Instead, she had turned to the window and was rubbing the grimy glass feverishly, trying to catch a glimpse of the receding platform. 'Of course,' he added, somewhat caustically, 'if you don't mind breaking your neck . . . '

'I don't see him,' she muttered, oblivious of his expostulations. 'You don't think he caught the train, do you? He wasn't far behind.'

'I should hardly think so,' he remarked dryly. 'You only just managed it yourself, you know.'

'Yes, of course.'

She bent for her case which had rolled

unheeded on the carriage floor. Picking it up, she placed it on the rack above the seats. Michael also stooped to pick up his magazine, which her precipitate entry had swept to the floor.

The train rattled out of the precincts of the rural station and into the darkness of the misty night. Outside, the mist-shrouded landscape sped by them like the passage of countless phantoms. The girl sighed as she pressed her nose to the cold glass of the window. It was still early evening, but it was beginning to get dark already. It always did once September had started. It would soon be time to put the clock back, too, she realised. And if there was anything she hated, it was that. To her, it meant another long winter in the office in London — a winter of rain and cold. Oh, how tired she was of having to live in London: seeing the same old faces, doing the same old work, taking down endless 'Yours faithfully' letters, and saying 'Yes sir' and 'No sir' to the pompous bosses of the company for which she worked. That was why she had travelled to the coastal town when she had a few days' break, hoping to snatch a few days' welcome change from routine. But it had all gone wrong . . .

She gave a deep sigh, subsiding into the seat again and settling back. Suddenly she gave a little gasp and sat bolt upright as a figure moved along the corridor. She said tremulously: 'Who's that?'

'Here, steady on,' urged Michael, leaning towards her reassuringly. 'It's only the guard — nothing to get alarmed about. Good Lord, you're as white as a sheet!'

'Yes, I know. I — I'm sorry.' She smiled faintly, self-consciously. 'I'm a little nervy, that's all. I'll be all right in a minute.'

'No you won't — not if you keep jumping like that,' he affirmed. He regarded her curiously. 'What's the matter? Something frightened you?'

The girl nodded.

'It was the man . . . following me!'

Michael stared.

'Following you? Where?'

'In the lane. Oh, it was nothing, I expect. Only — only it was a little alarming. And in view of what had happened previously . . . ' She pulled off her hat and shook out her hair in an effort to conceal her nervousness. 'I'm being frightfully stupid, I suppose.'

Michael was not so sure about that. He said enquiringly:

'Is that why you were running — because someone was following you?'

'Yes. That and because I wanted to catch the train.'

'Well, I'll be . . . ' Michael's curiosity got the better of him. He said practically, laying his magazine aside, 'Look here, I think perhaps you'd better tell me all about it. Then maybe I could help you.'

'Oh no, I couldn't bother you with my problems — I couldn't possibly,' she protested.

'Nonsense! Two heads are better than one, anyway. By the way, my name's Lane — Michael Lane. Now, then — ' He smiled reassuringly. ' — what's the trouble?'

The girl hesitated. Her custom being generally to treat strange young men who became so friendly with cold reserve, she found herself in something of a quandary. For somehow this young man was different.

He was plain and he was ordinary; but when he grinned you couldn't help feeling that he was a very sound and reliable person indeed, and you got the impression that if ever you were in a jam and needed someone badly to get you out of it, he was the man to do it. Not that she was in a jam, exactly — she could always return to Rockmouth and stay the night there — but she *was* worried, and although she couldn't see what in the world he could do about it, it would help to talk it over . . .

She told him that her name was Jill Shaw and that she was on holiday — or at least, she was supposed to be.

'It's rather stupid, really,' she went on. 'You see, I've just been to visit a relative I haven't seen for years. Only — only I can't find him.'

'You can't find him?' Michael raised his eyebrows. Surely it wasn't this that was worrying her?

'You see, I live in London,' she explained quickly. 'I haven't any parents — they died years ago, and the only surviving relative I have is Uncle Simon on the South Coast here. He's a seaman, I believe, though I'm rather vague about him — as I said, I haven't seen him for ages. Well, anyway, seeing that I was in the district for a day or two, I thought I'd look him up and stay with him overnight. I didn't bother to let him know: I wasn't sure whether I could make it, and in any case I thought it would be a surprise. But now — '

A frown darkened her face again, and her eyes held a puzzled, bewildered look.

'I could have sworn it was Pebble Bay where he lived, because I remembered thinking that time we went to visit him when I was a child what a lovely name it was for a fishing village. Besides, it was the same cottage — I'm sure it was. Yet when I arrived . . . he wasn't there.'

'You mean he'd moved?'

'Yes — no — I don't know. I don't know what to think,' she said confusedly. 'As his only relative, surely he'd have let me know if he had moved? I didn't hear from him often, I know: only about once a year — generally at Christmas time — but surely he'd have told me a thing like that? And yet . . . they said there was nobody of that name there at all — that there never had been.'

'They?'

'The people at the cottage.'

Michael nodded.

'I see. So what did you do then?'

'Do? I didn't know what to do. I thought I must have made a mistake: must have come to the wrong village or something. They're very much alike, these South Coast fishing villages, I believe. So I decided that there was nothing else for it but to make for the station again and go back to Rockmouth.'

She paused for a moment to collect her thoughts. Michael waited.

'It was getting dark by this time, and there was a mist coming up. I didn't linger — the village seemed deserted, and in view of what they had told me at the cottage, there didn't seem much point in enquiring further. Besides, I wasn't sure about the trains. So I made for the station as quickly as I could.' She hesitated. 'It wasn't until I'd reached the lane that I noticed I was being followed. Up till then

I'd thought it was only one of the villagers. But now I wasn't so certain, so to put it to the test I broke into a run.' She laughed a little, shakily. 'There was no mistake. I was being followed, all right — and had been ever since I'd left the cottage. I think it was when I realised that that I panicked.

'If there had been anyone else about, it wouldn't have mattered. But there wasn't — not a soul. That was why, when I was nearing the station and heard the train — ' She broke off and coloured a little. 'It was foolish, I know, but I had to dodge him somehow — I simply had to.'

Michael nodded understandingly. His eyes were thoughtful as he pondered a moment. He said suddenly: 'Look here, I suppose there could be no doubt that he was following you?'

'Doubt? How could there be? Giving chase like that — didn't it prove he was following me?'

'*Mm.* I suppose it did. All the same — ' He hesitated.

She looked at him questioningly.

'What's the matter? Don't you believe

me? Do you think I've imagined it?'

'No, no, of course not,' he assured her hastily. 'I was just wondering, that's all.'

'Wondering?'

'Wondering whether it couldn't all be capable of some simple explanation you haven't thought of.'

'But what simple explanation could there be?' she argued. 'People don't follow you for the fun of it. Neither do they tell you your uncle doesn't live where you expect him to live.'

Michael sighed.

'No, of course not,' he admitted. 'All the same — '

He fell silent for a moment, thinking the matter over. On the face of it, all she appeared to have done was to have made an error of judgment. Easy enough to mistake where a person lives, particularly when your last visit was when you were a schoolgirl. But however easily that part of the story might be written off, it in no way accounted for her claim to have been followed. Unless, of course, she *had* imagined it — as she had accused him of thinking — and her 'pursuer' had been none other than a fellow traveller on his way to catch the same train as she. The question was, was she that kind of a person? Michael, observing her covertly, decided she was not. There was something extraordinarily capable about that small, well-dressed figure that was sitting before him; something that ruled highly-strung hallucinations out of the question.

'Well?' She broke into his thoughts with an abruptness that startled him. 'What do you think?'

Michael did not answer for a moment. Then:

'I'm not sure,' he confessed. 'It seems to me that there are three possibilities. One: that you made a mistake and went to the wrong village, as you suggested yourself. Two: that you didn't make a mistake, and that you were told your uncle didn't live there because he didn't want to see you. Or, three: you were told he didn't live there because somebody else didn't want him to see you. That's how it strikes me.'

Her eyes widened.

'Oh! I'd never thought of it like that.'

She paused, then said suddenly: 'But it's ridiculous! Why shouldn't he want to see me? Or why should it matter to anyone else if he did?'

Michael shrugged.

'I wouldn't know. I'm merely putting it forward as a suggestion. Tell me, was he married — your uncle, I mean?'

She shook her head.

'He's a bachelor. He lives by himself — always has done. Why?'

'Nothing particular. I was only wondering. You see — '

He broke off as a sound came from the direction of the corridor; glancing up, they both saw the door slide open at the other side of the compartment, and the figure of a man appear on the threshold. Jill stiffened in her seat and half-started in apprehension, but a gesture from Michael calmed her again.

'Seats taken?' enquired the man, glancing about him.

Michael faltered noncommittally. 'Well — '

'They're not? Oh good.' The other seemed to take this hesitance in a manner contrary to what had been intended. He suggested civilly: 'Then perhaps you wouldn't mind if I shared your compartment? Train's quite full further up.'

'Not at all,' said Michael. He moved his magazine to his other side.

'Thanks.' The man stepped inside and slid the door shut carefully. Then, reaching up, he began to pull down the blinds overlooking the corridor.

'Like quietness when travelling,' he said, apparently sensing the surprised stares of his fellow-passengers. 'Less chance of being disturbed if you draw the blinds, you know.'

'Really?'

The other nodded.

'Has its other advantages, too,' he remarked, snapping the third blind into place. 'It prevents others from seeing what they shouldn't see.'

There was an odd note about the remark that made Michael stiffen perceptibly.

'Such as?'

'Such as this,' returned the other, turning to face them. 'No, sit where you are — both of you!'

Jill drew her breath in a frightened gasp

as she saw the automatic that was in the newcomer's hand.

Michael fell back in his seat, breathing heavily.

'Neat,' he commented. 'Very neat — what is this? Highway robbery, twentieth-century style?'

'No. Personal call on the lady, that's all,' replied the man with the gun laconically. He reached for the luggage-rack to facilitate his balance and edged further into the compartment. He said, looking at Jill: 'What were you doing at old man Shaw's cottage this evening?'

'What do you mean? I don't understand . . . '

'Don't you? I think you do. What did you want to see old Shaw for? Did he send for you?'

If the whole train had suddenly developed aeronautical powers and taken to the air, Jill could not have been more surprised.

'Send for me? Why should he?'

'That's what I'm asking you,' reminded the man with the automatic. 'Come on — speak up!'

Jill's astonishment lent her courage.

'Are you crazy? I tell you, I don't know what you're talking about.'

Evidently the man with the gun had not expected such obstinacy, for he glared at her savagely.

'You little fool! Bluffing won't help. I know you were at the cottage — I followed you from there! Why did you go? What did you want?'

Jill passed her tongue over her dry lips. Her breath came sharply, but she made no reply.

The man swore.

'Difficult, eh?' He moved towards her angrily. 'Why, for two pins I'd — '

Michael started from his seat involuntarily.

'Stop that — ' he began; but the other turned on him quickly.

'No, you don't!' he growled, adding ominously: 'I'm boss here; get down and keep quiet . . . or maybe I'll be tempted to make you!'

Michael hesitated for a moment, his eyes blazing. Then his gaze dropped to the automatic, and he sat back again, fuming. You can't argue with a gun — particularly with one that happens to be fitted with a silencer.

The other nodded approvingly.

'That's sensible. Now, then — ' He turned his attention to Jill again. ' — I want to know what you wanted with Simon Shaw. And I want to know quickly. You understand?'

'You're crazy!' she flashed. 'You must be! I don't know what you're talking about!'

The gun jerked suggestively.

'Come along — hurry up.'

There was a silence for a moment. Outside, the mist-shrouded landscape sped past them like the passing of countless phantoms. Within there was nothing but a monotonous swaying and clanking of wheels. Jill's eyes, looking across the compartment, sought Michael's; but his gaze was riveted to the gunman, steadily, implacably.

'I see. The stubborn sort, eh?' The man with the gun shifted impatiently. 'Well, not that it matters. Whatever you'd have said wouldn't have made any difference.'

Jill looked at him quickly. His smile was unpleasant.

'Too bad you should take it into your head to call on Simon Shaw tonight, isn't it?' he drawled. 'Because it means you'll have to be prevented from calling on anyone else — ever.'

'What do you mean? What are you going to do?' broke in Michael grimly.

'Put you both out of harm's way, that's all. Sorry if this lets you in for something that's not your pigeon, brother, but you can blame the lady for that: she should have chosen a compartment that was empty. You see, whatever she may have found out, she could have passed on to you — and that wouldn't do at all, would it? Besides, you might happen to have a good memory for faces, and I wouldn't want that!'

'You swine!' gritted Michael. 'Do you think you can got away with this?'

The smile broadened.

'I know I can. This little toy doesn't make as much noise as a pop-gun, and by the time they've found you, nobody'll know I've ever been on the train!'

There was no way out of it. Michael could see that.

Whatever happened now, it looked as though they were booked for a bullet . . . and Michael decided in one swift second that in that case he might as well meet his half-way.

Without the least warning, and in defiance of the automatic that was wavering between them, he sprang from his seat. It was the sheer audacity and unexpectedness of the move that made for its success. Lashing out for all he was worth, Michael's blow connected just a split second before the man with the gun snatched at the trigger, and as the startled gunman went reeling across the compartment to fall with a mighty thud against the sliding door, there was a soft plop and a ringing whine, and Michael felt something hot go whizzing above him.

Dazed rather than elated by his success, Michael turned to grab at the communication-cord. But before he could do so the train, puffing noisily and laboriously up a gradient, lurched violently, and taken unawares — for he was already slightly off his balance — Michael staggered backwards against the door. For a horrified moment he felt the door give . . . hold . . . then, with an ominous click which testified to the complete inadequacy of its catch, it flew wide open.

'Michael!' screamed Jill. 'Look out!'

She sprang from her seat in pure terror, but her cry was whipped away by the rushing wind. Leaping forward, she caught him by the arm as he toppled backwards; but his impetus proved too strong for her. The chill night air plucked at her like an angry demon; she had a kaleidoscopic vision of lights flashing before her eyes, and a dreadful sensation of falling. Then darkness leapt up to meet her . . .

2

Ghost Station

Why Jill did not lose consciousness during that terrible breath-taking fall from the crawling train, she never knew. Dimly, she remembered flying outward and downward through a world of darkness and flashing, until she brought up with a bump that shook every bone in her body and sent her rolling over and over in the damp grass by the side of the line. Dazed and shaking, hardly knowing whether she was dead or alive, she lay there gasping for a time until the clanking of the train had quite faded into the distance. Then all at once she heard footfalls somewhere near her and, struggling onto one elbow, she saw a dim figure look out of the grey fog that surrounded her on all sides like an impalpable blanket.

'Jill! Jill, where are you?'

She answered at once and the figure

turned; as it came running towards her, she saw that it was Michael.

'Jill! There you are! Thank God!'

He gave her a hand and helped her to her feet. She winced involuntarily and stumbled against him as a sharp pain ran through her ankle.

'What's the matter — are you hurt?' He held her tightly in an iron-like grip.

'No; only my ankle.' She was breathless and shaky and thankful for his support. 'I must have wrenched it a little as I fell, that's all.'

'You're sure it's nothing worse?' His tone was anxious. 'No bones or anything?' And as she shook her head: 'Thank goodness for that. For a moment I was afraid — What happened, anyway?'

'Don't you know? You staggered against the carriage door and it flew open. I — I tried to catch you, but — ' She shuddered. 'Oh, Michael — you might have been killed.'

'Me? You mean both of us,' he corrected. 'Even now I can't understand why we're not. Unless — of course, the fog.' His eyes gleamed with sudden understanding. 'We're damned lucky to be alive. Don't you see — it was the fog that saved us! If it hadn't been for the fog reducing the train to a mere crawl, and if it hadn't been climbing a gradient . . . ' His laugh was slightly unsteady. 'Shades of Dick Barton! I'd never have believed it!'

It was indeed as he had said. If there had been no fog, and the train had been travelling at its normal speed, then, whether they had been climbing a gradient or not, nothing could have prevented them being flung to destruction beside the track. As it was, all they had sustained were shakes and bruises — thanks to the inclemency of the weather!

Michael chuckled. 'I'll bet it gave Dick Turpin a shock! He's probably picturing our mangled bodies at this very moment. Quite an improvement on his original plan, wasn't it?' The mention of the man on the train brought a new furrow to his brow. He said curiously: 'What was the idea, anyway? What were you supposed to have found out? And what's all this business about your Uncle Simon?'

'Oh Michael, if only I knew. I simply

can't understand it . . . '

'It doesn't matter, anyway. Nothing matters at the moment except getting back to civilization.' He said, not very hopefully: 'You've no idea where we are, I suppose?'

'I haven't the faintest.'

He shrugged.

'Well, there's nothing to be gained by standing here. The best thing we can do is to set off and walk; if we follow the line long enough it'll bring us somewhere, I suppose. Can you walk?'

'I — I think so.'

'Lean on my arms. You'll find it easier going.'

He took her arm and they mounted the track; following the line, they ascended the gradient. The fog swirled about them eerily, its chill grey tendrils growing denser every moment. They spoke little during that strange trek through the blackness, for walking along the rough uneven sleepers proved difficult, and breath was precious. Gradually, however, as the pain in Jill's ankle eased and they became more accustomed to the short measured strides, they progressed steadily, the dull clip-clop of their heels contrasting strangely with an ever-present dull booming roar. Michael stopped.

'What's that?' he asked. 'That noise?'

'No need to get frightened,' said Jill. 'It's only the sea, I suppose.'

'You'll get frightened if you suddenly find yourself walking over the cliff top,' he reminded her grimly.

'Don't,' she begged, and shivered.

He grinned. 'Oh, no need to get frightened . . . '

But it was anything but a pleasant situation, thought Michael, as they made their way forward. They might walk on like this for hours before they came to a station. For, if he remembered rightly, stations were pretty rare on this section of the line, and he had a vague suspicion that they had chosen one of the loneliest stretches of the lot on which to fall.

The situation was bizarre in the extreme. Was the girl really as innocent of this peculiar business as she would have him believe? Or had the man on the train been right? Had she actually stumbled upon some knowledge he did not wish her to divulge? His mind boggled at the thought. Holy catfish! That would be pure Dick Barton! Still, it was odd, all the same . . .

How long his thoughts ran on in this strain, he never knew, but all of a sudden he came out of his reverie to find the girl plucking excitedly at his arm.

'Oh, look!' she cried. 'Look . . . ' His eyes followed the direction of her finger. Looming faintly in the swirling fog, a pair of gates barred the line.

'Is it — ?' breathed the girl.

'I don't know,' replied Michael cautiously. 'Anyway, we'll soon see. Think you can manage a bit faster?

But she had dragged herself free of his arm and was already running ahead of him, and he had to put on a spurt to catch up with her.

She was leaning on the gate when he reached it, her face radiant with relief.

'It *is*!' she cried exultantly. 'It *is* a level crossing! Oh, I'm so glad. Now we'll soon be at a station!'

Such an argument did not follow, and

Michael knew it. The popular belief that a level-crossing invariably meant a station nearby had as much chance of being proved false here as anywhere. But he nodded and helped her over the gate, and they had scarcely surmounted those on the other side of the road than a tall black building appeared with startling suddenness out of the fog.

'That's the signal-cabin, I suppose,' said the girl, breathlessly, stumbling along the weed-grown line. Then, almost before the words were out of her mouth, the grass by the side of the line changed to gravel, and they were hurrying up the gentle slope that led to the platform. But they had gone no more than half-way along the platform when suddenly Jill stopped. Something was wrong.

The colour died out of her cheeks, leaving them paper-white. She said, in a small, frightened voice:

'It's in darkness. The place is in darkness.'

Michael nodded. He hadn't been slow to realise that, either. Now he came to think of it, the gates at the level-crossing had been without their customary red lamps, and the signal-box, too, had shown no lights.

For some unaccountable reason, an odd thrill trickled up and down his spine. A screech-owl hooted mournfully in the dripping trees that hung darkly over the platform. The concrete, hardly visible in the gloom, felt strangely soft and resilient under their feet, and on bending down he found that it was covered with lush grass and tangled weeds which had grown unmolested between the numerous cracks. His grip tightened on the girl's arm as she gave a sobbing gasp. The station buildings — two or three mere huts in the mist before them — were utterly devoid of lights, and it wasn't natural.

'Steady,' he gritted, as much for his own benefit as for hers. She clung to him fearfully.

'Oh, Michael,' she tremored. 'I — I'm frightened. Why are there no lights? Where is everybody?'

She would have hung back, but he forced her to go on with him.

'I don't know,' he replied. 'Nothing to

worry about, though. Gas supply failed, probably. You know what those country places are like.'

It was absurd, and he knew that it was; but as she seemed to derive some comfort from the explanation, he let her think it. But it was not until they were quite close to the wooden structures that he realised how absurd the idea really was. Gas supply failed? Why, it didn't look as though the buildings had any gas supply connected. They were fairly crumbling away where they stood. He looked silently at Jill: she was trembling. Releasing his grip, he drew away from her and placed his shoulder against the nearest door. There was a protesting groan as it swung inward, then all at once the hinges gave way completely and the whole panel fell backward with a splintering crash.

Jill jumped.

A cloud of dust rose chokingly, only to be swamped in the swirling fog that eddied inward. Michael peered inside. It was dark out here in the open, but not so dark as the interior of what had been the station-master's office. Michael paused for a second; then, with a little exclamation, suddenly fumbled in his breast-pocket and pulled out a slim fountain-pen torch.

'I'd forgotten this,' he muttered. 'It's not too good, but it's better than nothing . . .'

He depressed the button. A faint, sickly radiance splashed the gloom and encircled the place. The walls were rotted. The floor was mildewed and damp. Huge black spiders scurried away from the light into the myriad of cobwebs that festooned every corner. Moving cautiously, Michael stepped inside, the girl following.

She gave a sudden choking cry, and he squeezed her hand reassuringly.

'Only a rat,' he said.

The sound echoed hollowly, and kept on echoing as they moved around. Their feet stirred the dust of ages on the floor. The dim ray stirred the shadows about them. But there was no sign of human habitation.

All at once, unsteadily, Jill said:

'Let's get out of here. Oh please, let's go.'

He was not sorry to do as she

suggested. He felt like that too. There was something horribly nauseating about the whole place. They passed out into the chilly night air with relief. She was grateful for the torch: without it, she would have panicked.

'What — what does it all mean?' she breathed. 'Surely all the place can't be like this?' She was dreadfully afraid.

'We can look at the other buildings if you like. There may be a chance . . . '

They did so by the torchlight, almost frantically, she clinging to him for courage. The wet trees rustled eerily on their right; the mist swirled and eddied in the ray of the torch; and above all, there sounded the dull muffled boom of the breakers — coming, as it seemed, from somewhere close at hand. It was hopeless, and they knew it. They knew before they began what they would find in the rest of the buildings. They were all alike: crumbling, rotting; empty, dark and silent. There was something incredibly sinister about that tiny station; something evil. It was against all the laws of the universe for there to be such a place. It was like a story-book, Michael reflected; only it was true.

For what seemed an eternity they stood there: two tiny humans facing each other in the creeping fog, with the deserted buildings standing out wet and dark in the ray of the torch, and the shivering trees gleaming darkly above them. Then Jill spoke, and her voice was so unnatural that she hardly recognised it as her own.

'Michael,' she whispered. 'Oh, Michael, am I dreaming, or is it — is this place — '

He nodded slowly.

'I'm afraid so,' he said. 'Yes, it's entirely deserted!'

3

Threshold to Terror

She took it more calmly than he had expected. The little colour which had returned to her cheeks during the excitement of their search ebbed swiftly away, and her breathing became a little quicker, but that was all.

She said:

'It can't be. It isn't possible . . . '

Her voice was deathly calm. There was something dreadfully unnerving about the silence of the place. Something that seemed to say: 'Keep away from here if you value your sanity'. It was absurd, of course, but — well, what *was* the explanation for the deserted station? Where was everybody: the station-master, the porters, the signal-man . . . ? It was unthinkable that the railway company should allow one of its stations to be so utterly empty and dark. Unthinkable that it should be allowed to fall into such decay. Especially seeing as it was on the Rockmouth-Pencastle line.

An icy finger stroked his spine.

He hadn't thought of it like that before. However small the place it served, this was a main-line station. It must be, for hadn't they followed the line after they had been thrown out of the train? Well, then? Oh, it was impossible . . .

He turned to the girl quickly.

'This place — have you seen it before?'

She shook her head, her lips pressed tightly together to keep back her growing terror.

'Never. Do you think I should be likely to forget it if I had?'

'But I thought you said you'd been in this district before?'

'So I have. But that was years ago — when I was a schoolgirl. All the same, I don't remember coming through a place like this — ever.' She looked at him, perplexity and worry writ large over her features. 'Oh Michael, do you think . . . '

'Think what?'

'I — I don't know,' she confessed.

'Only — only this place is horrible. It isn't real . . . '

'Now you're being silly,' he remonstrated. 'There's nothing to be afraid of.' He swung the torch round, but the fog, growing thicker every moment, threw back the beam in a sickly glare.

'It's no use trying to deceive me,' she said quickly. 'Goodness knows where we've got to.' She clutched at his arm. 'Oh Michael, let's go back the way we came. If I stay here much longer, I feel I shall go mad!'

'Go back? But that's absurd. We've come all this way, and now you're acting like a little child. I'll admit — ' He grimaced. ' — that this place doesn't look inviting, but at least — ' He broke off. 'What fools we are, standing here blithering when — '

'When what?' she asked, apprehensively.

'There ought to be a village somewhere, oughtn't there?' he went on. 'If there's a station, of course there ought. They don't plant stations in the middle of nowhere just for the fun of it!' He saw her face brighten in the back-glow of the torch. There was a new hope in her voice as she said:

'Then — then there's still a chance —?'

'Of course there is. We can get to know where we are. Food, shelter for the night — ' He caught her hand. 'Come along — we're wasting time.'

There was no need to tell her to hurry, for she was as eager to be off as he. Hastening through the tumbledown gateway that was the sole exit and entrance to the tiny station — the gate itself had long since rotted away — they found themselves in a rough, narrow lane.

Thick grass, long and tangled, lay underfoot, while hemlock and other weeds grew wildly in chaotic profusion. Rank, neglected hedges reared on either side with huge dark chestnut trees gleaming wetly in the sickly glimmer. And beyond, where the ray of the torch could not reach, the lane disappeared into the foggy blackness of the night.

Jill shuddered. It was like setting off to walk into nothingness; and even the prospect of finding food and shelter for the night failed to dispel the evil and horror of the place.

Resolutely, they plunged on. The only sounds that disturbed the unearthly stillness of the night were the mournful hooting of an owl and the muffled crash of the distant sea, with an occasional eerie rustle that seemed to start in the trees beside them and travel away into the distance.

'We shan't be long now,' said Michael, cheerfully. 'We might even be able to get a taxi.'

His voice went echoing faintly into the distance.

Jill did not answer; she tightened her grip on his arm and began to walk faster. But they had progressed no more than a hundred yards when suddenly it happened — and happened so horribly that they halted dead in their tracks.

From out of the night it came: a ghastly, bubbling scream, vibrant with agony, as if the person who had uttered it had all the devils in hell at his heels. It rose and fell in a hideous crescendo, carried with startling clarity by the sudden wind that blew towards them, and ending at last in a choking gurgle.

It was the cry of a man dying in pain — and dying horribly, violently. Michael muttered something under his breath. He had heard a cry like that before, and then it had been no accident. He began to run down the lane in the direction from where the sound had proceeded, Jill at his heels. At that moment the fog seemed to thin out somewhat, and the rising wind from the sea wafted it away as if a curtain had been lifted. A watery moon sailed out from behind the scudding clouds. Jill gasped.

'Look — in front!'

They had turned a corner and found themselves on the crest of a hill. The road — if such a track could be called a road — stretched down from their feet in a ribbon of whitish green into the valley below, to disappear into the huddle of thatched cottages that peeped out here and there from amongst the trees. Above them all rose a church steeple, and behind, the moonlit sea, gleaming darkly as it hurled itself against the crumbling cliffs.

Jill said thankfully, her sudden fear momentarily forgotten:

'It's the village. Oh, I'm so glad. Now we're saved.' She stopped close to Michael to regain her breath. But Michael did not seem to have heard her. He was gazing down at the village with a peculiar expression on his face — an expression so tense that she began to be afraid again.

'Oh Michael,' she said. 'What's the matter now? What was it — that noise we heard?'

He started.

'Noise . . . ? Oh, nothing — a bird, maybe.'

'You're lying,' she accused. 'Whoever heard of a bird like that?'

'Then maybe a steamer.'

'Or a steamer.' She looked at him. 'You're keeping something back from me. I know you are. What is it? What are you waiting for? Why don't you go down to the village?'

He shrugged, turning to her.

'You can go down if you like, Jill. But I shouldn't if I were you. Not if you don't want to waste time.'

'I — I don't know what you mean — '

He gestured towards the village.

'You've only to look. You don't need a telescope to see that the place is falling to pieces.'

The colour died out of her cheeks.

'I won't believe it!' she cried. 'It isn't true. The station — yes! But not this . . . '

She was stumbling blindly down the weed-grown road, telling herself that what he had said was not true: that in some way he was wrong. But the sight that met her eyes as she entered the village street shattered all her hopes. He followed her in silence as she ran first to one empty house and then to another, hoping against hope but fearing and finding the worst.

There were scenes of the wildest desolation: cottages with their doors hanging off on rusty hinges, huge, gaping holes in their roofs; shops, their windows long since shattered, their only inhabitants rats and spiders. The duck-pond, devoid of ducks and enlarged by the recent rains, came half-way across the grass-grown street; and even the church was in the same condition as the rest of the village. There was something tragic about the place.

The buildings seemed like mere shells, lonely and dead, hulked darkly against the moon, casting black shadows over the silver-washed streets. An air of gloom hung everywhere.

They hurried along the side streets, calling, exploring, but to no purpose. At last Jill stopped, all her old fears revived.

She was saying to herself:

'Deserted! A deserted village! No, no, I won't believe it!' She looked at him for confirmation. 'It isn't true, is it, Michael?'

He took her by the shoulders very firmly and looked her straight in the eyes.

'Look, my dear,' he said slowly, 'I'm afraid it is. It's no use deceiving ourselves. This place is as empty and as deserted as the station — God knows why.' Then, as a tiny cry escaped her, he added:

'Don't take it like that, Jill. It's nothing to get panicky about. However inexplicable it all is, there must be some explanation. Only we don't know it, that's all. The best thing we can do is to go back the way we came, and then — '

They had come to the main street again. The girl gave a little gasp and caught his arm.

'What — '

'The inn,' she breathed. 'Look — there's a light in it!'

He followed her gaze to a blackened building some yards along the street where a small chink of light gleamed from one of the lower windows.

'Funny. It wasn't there when we came. I'll swear it wasn't.' He frowned. 'Anyhow, come along — I think a look is indicated.'

It seemed an eternity before they reached the door of the place and pushed it open. Michael gave a call.

'Hello! Hello, there! Anyone here?'

There was no reply. Eerily, his voice echoed through the empty building. He switched on his torch, revealing a room stripped and decaying, a sight to which they were now becoming accustomed. A splintered counter marked what had once been the bar; empty shelves stood stark and lifeless. Away to the left was a closed door, from under which a faint gleam of light came filtering and crossed the floor, Michael moved towards it. Jill shuddered. He was turning the knob when suddenly she stopped him. He looked at her in surprise.

'What's the matter?'

'I — I don't know,' she admitted. 'There — there's something about this place I don't like.'

'Silly,' he chided her. 'If there's anyone here, they'll clear up the mystery for us.'

He threw open the door and crossed the threshold. 'Hello. Anyone here?'

He caught a glimpse of a rough deal table, the stump of a candle flickering in a bottle, and a shadow-cloaked figure bent over in a chair.

'Oh, good evening,' he went on. 'Sorry to butt in like this, but — '

He broke off. An icy chill ran through him.

Stepping forward, he placed his hand on the man's shoulder and shook it. There was no sound. No word. Only the sickening horror of seeing the head roll grotesquely to one side.

He had a hazy memory of what

happened next. Dimly he remembered Jill's screaming one anguished word — '*Uncle!*' — as she saw the sightless eyes and bloodstained features; seemed to hear once again that awful cry that had come out of the fog. Then he was bundling the girl out of the room and into the night again so that she would not see too much of that ghastly thing she called her uncle sprawling lifelessly over the table, its head all battered and covered with blood . . .

4

Hide and Seek

She was sobbing softly when he got her outside. True, she had no more than a glimpse of the man who lay there dead in the deserted inn, but what she had seen had proved to be the last straw for her overwrought nerves. All her defiant attitude was gone now. She looked what she was — a badly frightened girl.

Michael placed a comforting arm around her shoulder. She raised a tear-stained face and whispered:

'Oh, Michael — Michael, it was dreadful. My uncle . . . '

'Try not to think about it,' he advised her.

Michael's first sense of horror was quietly replaced by a wave of bewilderment. Even as he hustled the girl unceremoniously from that death scene, all that was logic and prosaic in him boggled at such an unlooked-for coincidence. That the poor devil lying there battered to death could be her uncle was impossible; she was shocked, overwrought — that was what it was. He said kindly as he got her outside:

'You're all right now. There's nothing to be frightened of. You've made a mistake, that's all. It can't be your uncle . . . '

'But it is, I tell you — it is!' She was sobbing unrestrainedly. 'Oh Michael, it's awful! It's Uncle Simon. And he's hurt — hurt terribly — don't you see? He needs help, and I've got to go back to him . . . got to . . . '

All at once he realised that she didn't know the truth; that she had grasped only half of it. He bit his lip. Had there been a faint possibility, he would have been glad to voice it. But he knew there was not. No man born could receive such horrible mutilation and remain alive. The only service he could perform was that of finding out how and by whom the blow had been delivered.

'No.' He grabbed at her arm as she made to go running into the inn again.

'You mustn't do that . . . Jill . . . do be sensible . . . please. It's not your uncle — how can it be? It's someone who resembles him, that's all it must be!'

She shook off his grip.

'But it is my uncle, I tell you — it is!' She was dragging away from him frantically, half-blinded by tears. 'Michael, you don't understand. Please let me go . . . '

'But — ' Doubt lingered in spite of her persistence. ' — are you sure — positive — ?'

'Of course I'm sure. Do you think I don't know my own uncle? I may not have seen him for years, but I'm not as dense as all that.'

She struggled past him.

'He's hurt, I tell you, and I'm going to him, and you won't stop me. Nobody'll stop me — '

And before he quite knew what had happened, she had brushed past him and was running into the inn again.

The truth hit him with the force of a blow, shocking him into action. Her uncle! Then he must stop her at all costs.

'Jill!' He plunged into the deserted inn

again and across the darkened tap-room, catching her by the arm before she had reached the door. 'Stop — do you hear? You mustn't go into that room. If he really is your uncle, there's nothing you can do for him — nothing anyone can do for him. *He's dead!*'

'What — ' She pulled up with a jerk, looking at him dumbly. She stared at him for a few moments, disbelief in her eyes. Then all at once she dragged herself free and darted towards the candle-lit room. Reaching the threshold she halted, staring fixedly at the sight beyond. Her fingers tightened on the edge of the door.

A sharp cry broke from her lips. No need to go any further: she could see only too well. No need for anything . . . now.

She felt Michael behind her as an unnameable something welled up within her, misting her eyes. Felt his arm about her waist, drawing her away. Dully, she allowed herself to be led out of the inn again. She knew Michael was talking, but not what he said; she knew nothing but an immeasurable horror that threatened to engulf her . . . Then gradually a great anger gripped her, douching her sorrow; a cold, fierce anger that filled her with determination.

'Michael — ' She choked back her tears. ' — whoever it was, we've got to find them — do you hear? Whoever killed Uncle Simon, we've got to find them!'

Michael nodded grimly.

'We'll find them,' he promised. 'Whoever was responsible for this night's work, we'll find them all right!'

He was remembering the man on the train; remembering what he had said about Jill being sent for. There was something odd here — something inexplicable. What was the connection between that incident and this? What was the mystery surrounding Simon Shaw anyway?

She was calmer now, and he was thankful. For one horrible moment he had thought she was going to have hysterics, but the moment had passed. He said however, just to make sure: 'Better now?'

She nodded.

'Good. Then if you'll stay here for a moment — '

She looked at him quickly.

'Why? Where are you going?' And then, as she divined his intentions: 'No, not back there! No, Michael, you mustn't!'

'But I've got to,' he returned. 'Don't you see, if we're going to do anything to avenge him, I've simply got to. I shan't be a minute.'

Once inside the cold fastness of the inn, Michael trod his way quickly across the tap-room again. The acrid smell of the dying candle greeted his nostrils as he entered the room, and the black shadows jumped spasmodically. He played the torchlight over the recumbent form that lay across the table.

He repressed a shudder at the sight of the face. It was not a pretty sight; quite obviously the man had been attacked viciously from behind, and battered to death almost before he had had time to resist. There was no doubt that he was dead; Michael realised what agony had brought forth those terrible cries. He rocked back on his heels and whistled softly. Which meant, of course, that lurking somewhere in the vicinity was a ruthless and dangerous murderer. It was a disturbing notion.

Michael gazed at the body thoughtfully. As near as he could tell, the dead man was about sixty years of age. Dressed as a seaman, with a rough woollen jersey and an old reefer jacket, his bearded face — what there was visible of it — was tanned by exposure to every kind of weather. His two hands, which lay tightly clenched across the table, were powerful and blue-veined, and his feet and legs were encased in a pair of huge thigh-boots.

Michael's examination took only a few moments, but was enough.

There was no doubt that he was Simon Shaw — the sundry letters found in his pocket proved that. But as to why he had been killed or by whom it had been done, there was no indication. Michael surveyed the figure ponderingly for a moment; then, blowing out the candle, he left the room.

'Jill!' he called softly as he stepped out of the doorway. 'Jill, I — ' He broke off in surprise and looked hurriedly around him.

Only the pale moon-washed street encountered his gaze. Jill was gone!

*   *   *

To say that Jill was not afraid when
Michael left her and disappeared once
more into the gloom of the inn would not
be true. Indeed, it would be a gross
misstatement. She was afraid — dreadfully so — and she herself was the first to
acknowledge the fact.

For a brief second she glanced towards
the cold blankness of the doorway and
heard Michael's footsteps rumbling beyond.
Then she turned away and curbed the
impulse that made her want to go running
in after him. He wouldn't be a minute,
he'd said . . .

She paced backward and forward in
the shadow of the inn, her every step
sounding crisp and clear in the uncanny
stillness. She wished her thoughts wouldn't
persist in going back to the dead man who
lay inside the inn. Thanks to Michael's
quickness, she hadn't seen much of the
body, it was true, but enough remained
in her mind to set her thinking deeply.
She, too, realised that it was a case of
murder . . . and there couldn't be a

murder without a murderer. The thought set her jangled nerves on edge again. It was like walking into the middle of a nightmare — fantastic, unreal.

Forcing it out of her mind, she looked about her. The street was silent and there was nothing to be seen. Only the faint shimmer of the restless waves as they reared and fell out on the sea, partly visible down the end of the street . . .

Suddenly, she stiffened.

A thrill of pure terror ran through her slender frame. Her heavy breathing almost ceased. Something dark and substantial was detaching itself from the engulfing shadows around her . . . something that was like a shadow and yet not like a shadow . . . something that to her startled eyes was huge and ominous . . .

She whipped round and tried to scream, but the cry was strangled in her throat as a coarse hand closed over her mouth. She struggled ineffectually as a strong arm encircled her waist, and the next second she felt herself being picked up and carried down the street . . .

What ghastly scar that nightmare

experience would have left on her mind had she remained fully conscious of it was never known, for at that moment outraged Nature took a hand. Her nerves that night had stood more than it was possible for them to stand. She knew nothing of the man who carried her so easily through the derelict streets of the deserted village. She knew nothing at all. She had fainted.

★　★　★

Michael stared about him for a few moments in utter bewilderment at the deserted street. Only the stark forms of the decaying cottages, wreathed in shadows, encountered his gaze. His mind whirled in a tumult of thought. Jill — where was she? What could have happened to her? That she had wandered off by herself was unthinkable: she was afraid of being alone, but she was more afraid of the village. Oh, what a fool he had been! Why had he left her? A dreadful fear clutched suddenly at his heart. Somewhere in this place lurked a murderer. Was it possible . . . ?

He was running down the street calling her name.

'Jill! Jill, where are you?'

A lone gull answered his call with a raucous screech, and his own voice came back to him in a mournful echo. Fearful, his inherent caution thrown to the winds, he hurried on.

'Jill! Jill!'

Rounding the corner at the end of the street, he found that it ended suddenly at the cliff edge. He pulled himself up with a jerk and stood panting and breathless, impervious to the fact that he might easily have taken a couple of steps too many. He was feeling nearly sick with worry. It was all his fault, too. If he hadn't been such a darned fool and left her by herself . . . She seemed to have disappeared utterly — as completely as if the earth had suddenly opened and swallowed her up.

The earth! He looked down as a loose piece of soil and rock crumbled under his feet and went shuddering down to the beach below. Suddenly, he started. There was a slight movement on the sand, and he strained his eyes. Wispy clouds, scudding across the moon, had turned the pale beach into a dirty grey, but he was able to make out the dark forms of two figures as they crossed the sand. His heart jumped. Could one be Jill? He dropped to his knees and shrank back into the shadows as he realised their direction. A narrow path twisted up the face of the cliff. They were already ascending.

Michael waited. Five minutes later, they were passing within a few inches of the crumbling wall behind which he was hiding, and his hopes were shattered. They were both men, and all they had with them was what appeared in the fleeting light to be a number of boxes. Breathless from their climb up the cliff, they passed him in silence. Michael slipped from his concealment and followed them along the road, crouching in every shadow. If they hadn't Jill with them, at least they might lead him to where she was . . .

His thoughts raced as he hurried along

in the wake of the silent men. Torn now between anxiety for Jill and a quickening curiosity, he would have given anything to have known who these men were. What on earth could they be doing in a place like this? he asked himself. What was in the boxes they were carrying? And what connection could they have with the man in the pub who had been so cruelly murdered?

His conjectures were broken off as the couple halted, and he realised with a start that he was back at the inn.

'Here, what's all this?' said one of the men, turning quickly to his companion. 'Look at this door — it's open!'

'So what? Maybe the girl did it,' retorted the other. 'This is where the boss found her, isn't it?' He gave a little laugh. 'Blimey, Slim, you're getting pretty jumpy these days, aren't you? What's coming over you?'

The man addressed as Slim scowled.

'Maybe there's something to get jumpy about,' he retorted. 'If you ask me, Steve, things aren't so hot. How much did the old man spill before the boss croaked him, I wonder? The boss says none, but I'm not so sure. Then there's this girl — the old man's niece, isn't she? How does she come to be here? I thought the boss sent Collins after her to keep her quiet?'

Steve nodded.

'So he did. And a blinkin' fine mess he seems to have made of it, also. Well, I wouldn't like to be in Collins' shoes when he gets back!'

The other grunted.

'That's Collins' lookout. What bothers me is who the girl's got with her.'

'But don't I keep telling you, we don't know that she's got anyone with her!'

'Then who was this bloke Michael she began babbling about, just before the boss gave her the dope to stop her coming round?'

'How should I know?' shrugged Steve. 'Maybe it's her boyfriend. Whoever it is, it doesn't mean to say that he's here.'

'No? I'm not so sure,' said Slim, doubtfully. 'Anyway, where's the girl now?'

'The boss is taking her to the ship,'

replied the other. 'Says he wants to question her.' He grunted. 'Waste of time, if you ask me. If she's seen what the boss thinks she's seen, he wants to get her dumped overboard pronto! Listen!' He paused. 'There he goes now.'

Faintly above the roar of the sea came the soft, rhythmical purr of a motor-boat engine. For a moment, it was all Michael could do to prevent himself running down to the beach to see, but somehow he managed to curb the impulse; and as he crouched in the shadows, his fists clenched.

'Come on,' grunted Slim. 'Let's take this stuff to the cache, then if you aren't satisfied, we'll have a look round to see if there really is anybody else. And if there is — '

His free hand moved suggestively towards his pocket, and Michael's eyes glinted. He knew what that gesture meant.

Michael breathed deeply as they disappeared into the inn. A momentary fear clutched suddenly at his heart, tempered by relief. The cold-blooded swine! At least Jill was safe: he knew that much. But for how long she would be safe was a different matter. What had they said? 'To the ship'? He came to his feet and slipped down the street again. So, there was a ship somewhere in the bay, was there? That was odd; he certainly hadn't noticed it. Then, as he reached the sea-front and saw patches of fog still hanging about the tiny harbour, he knew why.

His face was tense. If they were taking Jill back to the ship to question her . . . Ideas were buzzing in his head: grim, determined ideas. Somewhere on the beach should be another boat, he reckoned — that was, unless the thugs were going to stay ashore all night.

In that case . . .

He sought the cliff path and commenced his descent, scrambling down at a speed nothing short of suicidal. Every step he took, a gnawing fear clawed at his heart, and he prayed fervently that his assumption would not be unfounded. What sort of a racket he had stumbled upon, he could not guess, but he had seen enough to know that it was not pleasant. And when it came to keeping that racket dark, he knew that as they had committed one murder they would not hesitated at a second.

What guardian angel helped him to reach the sands in safety, Michael did not know; but reach them he did, and as he stood for a moment gulping in great lungfuls of air, his keen eyes scanned the moonlit expanse of wet beach that stretched out before him. A dark bulk stood close to the water's edge, and Michael's eyes gleamed as he saw it. It was a rowing boat.

He had scarcely reached it when a wild shout came echoing down from the cliff top. There was a whip-like crack and a shrill whine as a bullet thudded into the damp sand not a couple of feet away from him. The next second he was pushing off into the breakers which rolled huge and green on to the beach, and his attackers were left to blaze away at him to their hearts' content. He was well out of gunshot range by the time they reached the cliff foot; well out to sea.

Just where he was going, Michael did not know. His one purpose was to find

Jill, but before that he must find the ship. When he did, however . . . If Jill could have seen him at that moment, she would hardly have recognised him. His entire face was transformed. Ruthless, set purpose was depicted in every line of his youthful features as he promised several people, as yet unknown to him, various and unpleasant things.

And, what was more, at that moment he looked quite capable of carrying them out.

There was a heavy swell running and a stiff breeze blowing up, and although he was no seaman, it was obvious even to his unpractised eye that there was going to be a gale — and soon, too. A thick mist was falling over the bay again, shutting him in a world of his own — a mist that was growing denser as every second passed.

After a time, he paused, and shipped the oars to take a rest. As he did so, his eyes caught sight of a number of small objects in the bottom of the boat, and he reached out for one. It was a small package, carefully wrapped in brown paper, similar to the ones he had seen the men on the shore take to the inn. Michael looked at it for a moment, then snapped the string and tore off the paper.

A gleam of suspicion appeared in his eyes as he revealed a small metal container. Was it possible . . . ? He prised open the lid and whistled softly as he saw the shining white crystals beneath. Wetting his finger, he tasted one or two tentatively.

'Christ!' he exclaimed. 'Dope!'

5

Danger Ship

Jill came to with a splitting headache and a sweet, sickly taste in her mouth. The first thing she saw upon opening her eyes was a low, white-painted roof not three feet above her head. She was conscious, too, of a slight swaying motion, almost as though her entire surroundings were rolling from side to side. She tried to move her hands, but found that she was prevented from doing so by a strong thin rope that bound them tightly to her side.

For some moments she lay still, trying to collect her scattered thoughts and wondering where on earth she could be. She couldn't remember at first. She couldn't remember anything. Then all at once she did remember, and with the memory, quick dread surged over her. The man on the train . . . the deserted village . . . the lifeless figure of her uncle at the inn . . . the man who had seized her . . .

She twisted round on the small bunk on which she had been laid, and surveyed the room. It was small — pitifully small — with white-painted walls of panelled timber, and illuminated by a dim electric lamp swaying gently from the centre of the roof. In fact, it was rather like . . . Then she saw the porthole, and the motion of her surroundings became clear to her. It was not the first time she had been on a ship — seen a ship's cabin, even. It was not the first time she had been on the sea.

Jill kept her head admirably as she realised her position. How or why these things were happening to her, she didn't know. She knew only that, whether she liked it or not, she had landed herself into a mess far stickier than she had ever experienced in her life. If only she hadn't been such a simpleton and remained outside the inn! She wondered what Michael had said when he had discovered that she had gone. Probably she would never know . . .

She shivered. It was not a pleasant position. That she was in the hands of the man — or, rather, men; for she knew enough about the sea to appreciate that the boat on which she was captive was too large to be handled single-handed — who had been responsible for the murder of her uncle was obvious. The only thing that puzzled her was why it had happened at all. What was their game? And how had Uncle Simon come to be mixed up in it, anyhow? That it was something nefarious, that it was something they were anxious to keep dark, was clear. And when they had murdered once . . .

She pulled herself up with a jerk. No use crying before the milk was spilt. That would get her nowhere. To keep her mind from this unpleasant and gruesome subject, she fell to wondering what exactly their game was, and the only solution at which she could arrive was smuggling. She almost laughed. Impossible. People didn't smuggle these days. At least, not in real life. It was too much like a storybook . . . But then, so was the present situation, she realised. Mysterious

67

men . . . deserted villages . . . murder
. . . There she was again. Couldn't keep
her mind from murder. Far better occupy
her mind in trying to get free . . .

She became aware all at once that there
was a sound at the door, and as she
turned to face it, she caught her breath.
The next second, there was the click of a
lock and the door swung inward; in the
uncertain light, she saw a man cross the
threshold and move towards her. He
grinned slowly, bent over the bunk, and,
with as little effort as it would have taken
him to have lifted a kitten, picked her up
and carried her from the cabin. There was
a strong scent of spirits about him that
even the chill wind on the deck could not
disperse, and her eyes opened wide with
alarm and apprehension as she gasped:

'Where are you taking me?'

'You'll see,' answered the man, cryptically. 'And in the meantime, I wouldn't
advise you to try screaming or anything
like that. The boss doesn't like it. It
wouldn't do you any good, anyway,' he
added with a crooked smile. 'Nobody'd
hear you.'

Jill struggled in his powerful grasp, but he merely chuckled, and presently they stopped outside another cabin further along the companion-way, the door of which he opened by the simple expedient of a kick from his hefty boot. The room into which she was taken swam thick with the blue haze of tobacco smoke, and through it she glimpsed half-a-dozen of the toughest-looking characters she had ever seen. They were lounging indolently in chairs around a polished mahogany table, a couple of bottles of whisky and a cluster of glasses standing near at hand — recent contributions, no doubt, to the general air of inebriation which prevailed.

'Ah, good evening, young lady!' said one of the men nearest her. He rose to his feet with mock courtesy as she was brought in and dumped unceremoniously into a chair. 'We're feeling quite honoured. Female visitors are quite a rarity round here. This sure is an unexpected pleasure.'

Jill took a dislike to him immediately. She thought all at once of a life-sized and repulsive beetle, and the simile was admirable. He had a fat, swarthy face and small pig-like eyes, and a round, fat body that was grotesquely over-dressed. Presumably he was the leader, for he appeared to be the only one who was sober. He smiled at her in a manner which no doubt was intended to inspire confidence. If such was the case, it failed deplorably.

The revulsion she felt brought with it a spurt of anger. She said:

'Not for me, it isn't!' And then, realising that only through her anger could she hide her fear: 'What do you mean by all this? Why have you brought me here? Why have you tied me up? What do you want?'

'The pleasure of your company, my dear,' purred the other. 'Just for a little while — that's all.'

'Oh, you brute!' she cried. 'Just wait till I'm free! I'll make you pay for this — all of you. And when I do — '

'When?' The big man chuckled, and there was no mistaking the meaning of that sound. An unnameable something stroked Jill's spine.

'What do you mean by that, you brute? What do you mean . . . ?'

70

The human beetle reached for a chair and pulled it towards him, straddling it backwards and leaning towards her, his hands on the rail. His eyes narrowed to mere slits that were almost lost in the wreaths of fat surrounding them. He said, very quietly:

'Simply that I don't think there'll be a 'when'. You know too much, my dear; and you know what happens to people who know too much, don't you?'

'I — I don't understand,' she faltered, shuddering.

'Don't you? I think you do, you know.' He said suddenly: 'Who sent for you? Who was it?'

The boat heaved in the rising swell, and Jill's head ached to splitting point. She said faintly:

'*Sent* for me?' Her surprise was unbounded. 'I don't know what you mean. No one sent for me. Why should they?'

'Who sent for you?' he repeated.

'But I've just told you. No one sent for me. I haven't the faintest idea what you're getting at.'

'No?' rasped the other harshly, all

71

pretence of geniality disappearing from him in a flash. 'I think you have — Miss Shaw.'

'Miss — ?' The use of her name surprised her, and she caught her breath.

The man smiled.

'You aren't going to deny that you are Miss Shaw, are you? You aren't going to deny that you're the old man's niece, and that you called at his cottage this afternoon asking for him? You aren't going to deny that, are you?'

Jill didn't answer. There was no answer to give. The man nodded.

'Very sensible, I'm sure. I only hope you're going to be as sensible about everything else.' He said suddenly, going off at a tangent: 'Who did you bring with you?'

Jill started.

'No one,' she denied. 'No one at all.'

'No? Then who's Michael?'

'Michael?' She tried her hardest to look blank. Was there nothing they didn't know?

'Yes, Michael,' retorted the fat man. 'Who is this boyfriend of yours? Where is he?'

'Are you crazy?' she demanded. If they knew so little about him as to be so insistent as this, she was certainly not going to help them. 'I don't know what you're talking about. I don't even know a Michael.'

The man smirked.

'Don't be stupid, my dear. You spoke quite a lot about this Michael chap just before you came round. Where is he?'

'I've already told you,' gasped Jill. 'I don't know.'

'No? Think again, my dear.'

'I — I — ' Her head throbbed as if about to burst. Her words stuck and she floundered helplessly.

The man grinned. He said unpleasantly:

'Never mind, my dear, it doesn't matter. The boys are in the village, so I expect they'll take care of him, whoever he is.'

For an awful moment Jill thought her heart would cease beating altogether. Her own terror faded; stark fear for Michael took its place. She had no delusions as to what 'taking care of' implied.

'You wouldn't . . . dare!' she breathed.

'Wouldn't we?' The big man chuckled as he came to his feet. A fleshy hand dipped into his pocket, and came out again gripping a small, blue-barrelled automatic pistol. 'You'd be surprised what we'd dare!'

Something cold gripped Jill's heart. She said, chokingly:

'You mean — murder? You mean you'd commit murder again?'

'*Again?*' It was like the firing of a starting gun. The fleshy man leaned forward eagerly, his eyes gleaming. 'So you did see it? You did go into the inn? Lady, that's all we want to know. You *have* seen too much.'

Jill choked. Too late, she realised how indelibly she had sealed her own death-warrant. Panic seized her. Her thoughts whirled in chaotic confusion. She said hurriedly:

'No, I didn't. I didn't see anything . . . I couldn't . . . '

'No? Why not?'

'There wasn't time . . . and he wouldn't let me, anyway . . . He . . . Oh!'

74

She stopped suddenly, biting her lip. Her colour ebbed away in consternation. The man smiled grimly.

'He wouldn't let you, wouldn't he? Who wouldn't — Michael?'

'No. I didn't mean that at all.' She made a vain effort to retract her words. 'I meant only — '

'My dear Miss Shaw, it doesn't matter what you meant — now!'

Jill stared at him for a few moments in stupefaction. Then her stricken gaze dropped to the cold bulk of the pistol, she heard a tiny click as a podgy thumb snapped back the safety-catch, and she saw a flash of blue as the automatic spun neatly in the stubby fingers. 'I don't know where you've come from or what you're doing here, but it seems pretty clear that you've seen more than is good for you. And in that case . . . ' He let the sentence trail off suggestively.

'You mean you're going to . . . murder me?'

'Come, now, don't call it murder,' the fat man protested, smiling. 'Let's just say *putting you out of the way*, shall we?'

75

'You swine!' Jill gasped, struggling vainly with her bonds.

'Boss,' came the plaintive voice of one of the gang, 'let's get on and give her the works. I — I don't feel too good with this boat rockin' like it is.'

The fat man cast a contemptuous glance across the table.

'Tobacco and whisky,' he snapped, 'you fool! You'll be seasick before we get to France. I told you to lay off that stuff. There's a storm coming up, too.'

The man groaned, and his pasty countenance turned a shade greener. The leader swept a glance over his companions. One or two of the others weren't looking too good, either. They were getting restive at the inaction, and he knew it. He heaved his great bulk resignedly from the chair, and turned again to Jill.

The girl shrank back from him as he approached.

'Keep away from me!' she screamed.

'Sorry, lady, but I can't oblige,' he mocked. The gun in his hand moved upwards towards the level of her eyes. 'I rather hate to do this,' he said in feigned regret, 'but as I said before, you know too much, and that isn't good for you. Guess I can offer you one consolation, though. You can rest easy in the knowledge that your boyfriend will be well taken care of too.'

His eyes were hard, merciless. 'Goodbye, my dear. It's been nice knowing you!'

His finger tightened on the trigger.

★ ★ ★

To Michael, the night seemed to be one of never-ending surprises. First of all, the man on the train; next, the deserted village; then the body in the inn; after that, the disappearance of Jill . . . and now this. He sat for a moment, gazing at the small packages of cocaine which lay in the boat. So that was the secret for which the men in the village had been prepared to commit murder? That was the secret they were so anxious to keep to themselves? They were drug-smugglers! His mind reeled.

It didn't seem possible: it was too fantastic to be real. He felt that at any minute he would wake up and find himself in the railway carriage. Yes, that was it — he was dreaming. He had been reading too many sensational novels, and the consequence was that these impossible adventures were taking possession of his dreams. Simple explanation . . .

But when a large wave came sweeping over the gunwale of the boat, he realised that he was not dreaming at all. Indeed, he was very much awake, and drenched to the skin. With a start, he looked round. The thick fog curled about him like a blanket. The moon had disappeared completely, and the beach was invisible. He picked up the oars and began to row again, then discovered that he had lost his sense of direction altogether. The swell was running rapidly now, and it was as much as he could do to keep the boat afloat, let alone steer it. God! He'd as much chance of finding the ship in this sea as . . .

Wait, though! What was that out to port? The fog shifted a little as the wind veered, and a tiny pinpoint of light came twinkling out of the darkness. Michael breathed heavily. Of course. The ship would have to show some indication of its position for the benefit of the men in the village. He gave thanks to heaven for that saving glimmer, and set off rowing for it as fast as he could.

It was hard work in that rising gale, and though Michael put every ounce of strength he had into it, it was fully ten minutes before the little boat finally scraped under the lee of a trim motor-yacht which was riding at anchor in the bay. It took him another two precious minutes to find the rope-ladder by which he could climb up the side, but at last he did so, and it was not long before he found himself standing breathlessly but firmly on the ship's deck. A small glimmer of light escaped from the corner of a nearby hatch-cover, and he moved silently towards it.

A murmur of voices came to him as he lifted the tarpaulin and peered below. He saw two men.

'Beats me why the boss doesn't push off,' he heard one grumbling. 'With this swell running, I feel a bit queer in the stomach. What the hell is he waiting for, anyway?'

'Some of the boys are still ashore unloading the snow,' returned his companion. 'We've got to wait for them, haven't we? Besides,' he went on, 'the boss wants to grill the girl first, and find out what she was doing snooping around the village. If she really is old man Shaw's niece and he sent for her, there's no telling what she might have found out.'

The other grunted.

'Then I wish to goodness he'd get on with it, that's all.'

Michael breathed deeply. So he wasn't too late after all? At least she was alive . . . He had no time to listen further, however, for as a heavy footfall sounded across the deck, a harsh voice rang out:

'Hey, you!'

Michael swung round in time to see the unbeautiful figure of a dirty sailor coming towards him. It was the surprise tactic that did it. For without a single warning or thought for the consequences, Michael flung himself forward and sent a sharp right crashing to the other's chin. There was a painful gasp as the sailor went staggering across the deck, and the next second Michael was on top of him. There was no time for resistance. A couple of punches in well-selected places, and the would-be antagonist left this world for the quietude of the unconscious — where Michael considered he was likely to remain for some time.

Michael stood up and wiped his knuckles. Another few seconds and it might have been sticky . . . With unhurried swiftness he ran his hands over the human log . . . and as a reward came to his feet with an automatic pistol in his hand. Michael grinned as he slipped it into his pocket. The odds were not so uneven now.

He had just pulled Sleeping Beauty into concealment behind the hatch-cover when footsteps sounded again, and the next second he saw the two men from below come climbing on to the deck. Michael drew back.

'I reckon we'd better go an' see if the girl's come round yet,' remarked one. 'If she hasn't, we look like being anchored here all night!'

His voice trailed off as it was snatched

away by the wind, and the two moved across the deck. Michael followed, feeling jubilant. At last he was going to find out where Jill was being kept a prisoner. So the boss was going to question her, was he? He hoped, for the boss's sake, that she hadn't been harmed. If she had . . . After his successful encounter with the first of the ungodly, Michael was feeling good, and simply itching to repeat the performance.

A thin streak of light cut across the deck as the men opened a cabin door and passed within. It was closed again before Michael had time to reach it, and he was just about to creep towards it when another door opened further along the companion-way, and footsteps sounded once again.

He heard a voice say: 'Where are you taking me?'

Michael froze. It was Jill.

His face set, he watched her as she was being carried into the cabin, and the door had barely closed behind them than he was up to it and peering through the narrow slit in the curtain that covered the window. Through the small space he saw her being dumped in a chair, and one of the men rise mockingly towards her. And then he gasped. For he recognised the large, fat face and the repulsive smile.

It was 'Tiny' Peters. The man whose hideous countenance had been splashed over every newspaper in the country. The man who was wanted by the police for practically every crime in the calendar, including murder.

Tensely, he watched the scene as it was enacted within. He could hear no words beyond a faint murmur, but he knew as well as if he had been inside himself what was being said. And he also knew the position.

Suddenly he stiffened, his blood running cold. He saw the flabby form of Peters rise ungainly from the seat and move towards Jill. He saw the stubby automatic in Peters' fist elevate to the level of her eyes. And in that awful second, too, when he saw the crook's finger tighten on the trigger, Michael acted.

As one hand went for the handle of the

cabin door, his other went for his pocket. The next second the door was wrenched open, and he was stepping inside.

6

Tables Turned

Jill was never able to fully tell her thoughts in that terrible moment when the Angel of Death rustled its chill wings over her. She was brave — Peters himself had acknowledged that — but even the bravest cannot look with equanimity down the barrel of a Browning automatic when the trigger is being depressed. In that brief moment when the fat man's finger tightened on the trigger, she died a thousand deaths. She wanted to scream, but she couldn't; her tongue cleaved to the roof of her mouth, and her vocal chords refused to function; she heard the slow, drawling words of the man who was the boss, and saw the look on his merciless face. And as a cold shudder broke her frame, she closed her eyes and prayed that it would soon be over.

And then it happened — a thing so

sudden and unexpected that it momentarily paralysed everyone in the cabin. There came the sound of an opening door, a sharp report . . . and the gun in the boss's hand was whipped away as if by magic.

Jill wilted as she heard the shot; waited for the sharp impact of the bullet. But it never came. Instead, the voice she knew so well rang through the cabin like the crack of a whip.

'Stay where you are — all of you! The first man who moves gets it!'

Jill gasped and opened her eyes. In the open doorway she saw a tousle-headed young man covering the dazed gangsters with a business-looking automatic.

'Michael!' she exclaimed, and there was a world of relief and incredulity in her voice.

Michael grinned.

'Hello, Jill,' he said. The next second, he had turned his gun towards the snarling gangster, who was sucking his fingers painfully. 'Now then, Peters, set her free,' he commanded, his eyes like twin chips of ice.

Peters stared.

'You know me?' he gasped. 'How — ?'

'After all the publicity you've had, I should think nearly everyone in the country knows you, you rat! Come on, get a move on. You heard what I said — set her free. And by heaven, if you've harmed so much as a hair of her head . . . '

For a big-time racketeer, Tiny Peters was unusually submissive. With a fierce scowl which should have withered anyone less imperturbable on the spot, he moved sulkily towards Jill and began to untie her bonds. But as the last strand fell to the floor and the girl came unsteadily to her feet, he grasped her suddenly by both arms and swung her round so that she covered him like a shield. There was a gleam of triumph in his eyes as another automatic sprouted in his fist. But his triumph was only short-lived, for Jill was slim and he was big, and his automatic barked only once . . . then clattered to the floor as Michael fired with unerring accuracy. In a flash, Jill had wrenched herself away from the cursing thug's grip and had run to the doorway. She had flung her arm round Michael and was sobbing thankfully on his shoulder.

'Michael, oh, Michael!'

'You're all right now, my dear,' he assured her. He motioned towards the glaring crooks again. 'Another move like that, and I'll down the lot of you,' he promised. 'Got it? Right, then. The next move is to throw your artillery on the floor, then file through the door one by one like good little boys. And,' he added, as they hesitated, 'I'll give you just two seconds to do it.'

They were quick enough after that. Even a schoolboy could have gained their respect had he possessed such firing ability as Michael's. Leaving a small pile of weapons behind them, six grim and bewildered crooks filed meekly from the cabin. Watched as if by a tiger, the unhappy band were marched sullenly to the forward hatch, and within a few minutes they had been battened down safely below . . .

'Oh, Michael!' cried Jill suddenly, catching sight of his arm, and there was a note of fear in her tone. 'You — you're hurt . . . '

He glanced at his shoulder where an

ugly red patch was beginning to spread through his jacket.

'Only a scratch,' he assured her cheerfully, although the wound was beginning to hurt like fury. 'Nothing to worry about so long as you yourself are all right. They didn't harm you, did they?'

'Oh no,' she replied. 'Only . . . ' She shuddered. 'If you'd come a moment later . . . '

'But I didn't come a moment later,' he said comfortingly, 'so you're not to think about it.' He slipped his gun into his pocket and put his arm round her shoulders. 'We've got this gang bottled up nicely now, and as the others are stranded ashore, it looks as though we've got possession of the craft entirely. But just in case there are any more, I'm going to scout round, so you'd better wait for me in the cabin.'

'No I hadn't,' she said determinedly. 'I'm coming with you. I don't want to lose you a second time.'

Michael grinned.

'Would that have mattered so much?' he asked her.

'Maybe — maybe more than you realise,' she answered in a low voice.

'Miss Shaw, seeing we only met a few hours ago, that's a pretty rash statement to make.'

It was doubtful whether she heard him, however, for the wind was howling furiously now, lashing the sea to a frenzy. Unsteadily, they crossed the deck and made their way towards the bridge. It took them all their time to reach it, but at last they did, and as they approached the wheelhouse, Jill gripped his arm.

'Look, there's a light — there's somebody there!'

Michael nodded. Even as they watched they saw a movement across the lighted panel of the wheelhouse door. Creeping towards it, Michael turned the handle, and with infinite caution pushed open the door and peered inside.

Through the small opening he glimpsed the bent figure of a man poring over some papers. Quite obviously it was the captain, and so engrossed was he that he had not the slightest inkling of his danger — until he felt the hard muzzle of Michael's gun touch the back of his neck.

His reaction was instinctive. Slowly, he raised his arms, the colour receding from his florid face.

'Make one sound,' breathed Michael, 'and you're a dead man!'

'Who — who are you?' whined the blue-coated figure, turning slowly to face them. 'The boss'll have something to say about this . . . '

'The boss has said all he's going to say,' Michael informed him sardonically. 'Just now he's out of circulation, so you'd better do as I tell you or take the consequences. Where's the mate?'

The captain remained silent, eying Michael truculently. Michael's gun extended and prodded him gently in the ribs.

'He — he's in the engine-room,' replied the other, hastily. 'Awaiting orders to push off.'

'Anyone else?'

The gun barrel went into operation again.

'A couple of engineers.'

'Right,' said Michael. 'Now we know where we are. How long do you think it'll take to get this craft moving?'

'I — I don't know,' said the man, thoroughly scared. 'The engines will want starting. Besides, there's a gale springing up . . .'

'Never mind about the gale,' retorted Michael. 'We're sailing as soon as possible. Tell the men below to up anchor and start the engines. And by heaven, if you give them one hint that I'm here — '

'But — '

There was no 'but'. The menace of the automatic and the expression on Michael's face saw to that. Turning towards the engine-room telegraph, the captain picked it up and gave out the necessary instructions.

'Well,' he said at length, replacing the receiver, 'what do you want me to do now?'

'Make for the nearest port,' replied Michael.

The captain blanched.

'I can't do that, you fool,' he protested. 'We'll all be gaoled, with the stuff we've got aboard.' He eyed Michael suspiciously. 'Who are you, anyway? A copper?'

'Maybe,' said Michael cryptically. If the

other supposed that, it was as well to let him go on thinking it. 'Who I am doesn't matter just now. I'm ordering you to sail for the nearest port immediately!'

The captain licked his dry lips. There was wild fear in his eyes as he looked between Michael and Jill.

'I'll see you in hell first!' he shouted. 'You bloody fool, do you think I'm going to commit suicide?'

'You'll do as I say!' snapped Michael. 'And — '

He broke off as the captain, mad with fear, launched himself forward. It was a crazy move. Even as he leapt, Michael hit him scientifically with the butt of his gun, and he sank to the floor without a murmur. Michael looked at him regretfully.

'Worst thing that could have happened,' he muttered. 'I was afraid I might have to do that. I suppose you wouldn't know anything about navigation, would you?' And, as Jill shook her head, 'Neither do I. Which means we'll have to wait till he comes round, that's all . . . Wait a minute, though!' His eyes gleamed as an idea came suddenly to him. 'Of course!

Why didn't I think of it before?'

'Think of what?' asked Jill.

'The radio!' said Michael. 'There's bound to be a radio on board, isn't there? Very well, then, what's to prevent us signalling to the coastguards with it?'

'Nothing — if you know how to use the thing.'

'Of course I know how to use it!' Michael cried. 'Radio's a hobby of mine — always has been. Come along . . . '

'Here, hold on a minute,' said Jill, grabbing his arm. 'What are we going to do with him?'

'Him? Oh, yes!' said Michael, smiling at the unconscious figure she had indicated. 'That's one up to you, Jill. We mustn't leave him to kick up a row, must we?'

By the time they had finished with him, the unconscious captain was not in a position to do anything. With his own handkerchief covering his mouth and two pieces of stout rope round his ankles, he had as much chance of getting free as he had of flying.

'There,' said Michael, eying their handiwork with satisfaction. 'That should keep him quiet. Come on!'

They had no difficulty in locating the radio cabin. Opening the door, they found, as they had expected, that it was unoccupied, and together they slipped inside.

It was the work of a minute for Michael to don the earphones and switch the transmitter into life. Spellbound, Jill watched him. There seemed to be no end to the surprising qualities he possessed. The small cabin became filled with the tick-tick of the tapper as rapid streams of Morse were sent into the ether. That those strange little taps could make sense seemed absurd; yet Jill knew, even as she listened, how much depended on their reception. At last it was finished, and Michael sat back with a sigh of satisfaction.

'That's that,' he said, removing the headphones. 'There's been no reply, so I only hope somebody heard it. All we can do now is wait.' He rose to his feet. 'Come on, Jill, we'd better get back to the wheelhouse and see how the captain is.'

The wind shrieked demonically as they

stepped on to the deck again, and the ship heaved in the grip of the mighty waves. Jill shivered as she clung to Michael's side, and together they hurried towards the protection of the wheelhouse. They never thought of danger, and it was only the merest premonition that came to Michael as he opened the door. It was instinct more than anything else that made his hands fly to his head. But he was too late, for the savage blow struck him fairly on the skull.

In one blinding flash he realised his mistake; realised what a fool he had been to forget about Sleeping Beauty, whom he had left in the shadow of the hatch-cover. Then a million flaming lights danced before his eyes, and something seemed to explode within his brain; and the last thing of which he was aware before consciousness left him was Jill's frightened scream — coming, it seemed, from a great distance. Then he knew no more.

7

Nightmare!

For the second time that night, Jill awoke to find herself a prisoner. The same unpleasant sickly taste pervaded her mouth as it had done on the previous occasion, and she felt ill, mentally and physically. Of what had happened after the man had stepped out from behind the door and attacked Michael with a heavy spanner, she had no clear impression. She remembered herself screaming, and she remembered herself running wildly across the deck. She remembered, too, the jar with which she had cannoned into something in the darkness. But after that . . . nothing.

She could only guess that she had been drugged.

How long ago that had been was also a mystery. It must have been some considerable time since, however, for the ship was now rocking violently, and the shrieking of the wind as it lashed the sea into a frenzy indicated that the threatened storm had at last burst.

Her heart sank as she reviewed the prospects. Things certainly did not look very bright. That Michael's S.O.S. had been picked up she could not believe, for help would surely have been to hand by now. Besides, what chance of rescue was there on a night like this? And who was to tell their present position anyway? They might even be well out to the open sea by this time.

She listened intently. The engines were silent. That meant that they were not moving, at any rate. The thought gave her hope. Of course. A captain who knew his job would hardly set sail in the teeth of a storm like this . . .

A low groan close to her cut suddenly across her thoughts, and with a start she looked round. At first, the bent figure huddled horribly on the floor amid the shadows not a couple of yards away from her made her shrink back — until it opened its eyes and glanced up at her.

'Michael!' she exclaimed.

Michael grinned — or at least tried to.

'Hello, Jill,' he said weakly.

Her heart leapt as she looked at him. The sight he presented was not exactly one to gladden the eyes. His face was cut and he was grimy. A trickle of blood showed through his tousled hair where he had been hit with the spanner. His shoulder had stopped bleeding, but his jacket was stained by coagulated blood. He was bound by the hands as she herself was, but somehow he managed to wriggle round so that at last he was facing her.

'Oh, Michael!' she exclaimed tearfully. 'You're hurt!'

He dismissed the fact with a shake of his head. 'Where — where are we?' he asked her.

She smiled at him ruefully.

'We're still on the ship, I'm afraid. Only this time it's us who are down in the hatch, and not the gang of crooks.'

'I see.' He laughed bitterly. 'This is what comes of being so darned clever, I suppose. Sorry, Jill, but you see this is my fault.'

'Your fault?'

'Yes. When I came aboard, the first thing I met was trouble in the shape of one of the crew. Before he could raise the alarm, however, I knocked him cold and left him sleeping peacefully behind the hatch-cover. Then, like the fool that I am, I forgot all about him. So you see, you've got me to thank for this pickle.'

'Michael — ' She laughed shakily. ' — don't be an ass! If it's anyone's fault, it's mine — for imposing myself and my troubles on you in the first place. If it hadn't been for me, you'd never have got into this mess: never have known anything about it.'

'Oh, rot!' he said gruffly.

'But it's true,' she declared, 'and you know it's true. If I hadn't been such a fool and accepted their cock-and-bull story about them not knowing Uncle Simon; if I'd gone to the police as I ought to have done . . . well, things might have been different. Michael — ' She looked at him quickly. ' — we're in a tough spot, aren't we? No, don't try to disguise it,' she went on as he opened his mouth to protest. 'I

100

know what class of men they are. We'll be lucky to get away with our lives, won't we?'

'Oh, I wouldn't say that . . . ' he began comfortingly.

'They've murdered once to keep their secret — whatever it is — and they'll do it again. I know they will. And unless something happens — '

She broke off as the hatch-cover opened suddenly above them, and two burly seamen in glistening oilskins came clambering down the ladder. Jill watched them apprehensively, wondering what was going to happen next. She had not long to wonder, for the next minute they were both being carried aloft.

They gasped as the full force of the gale smote them, and after being carried some distance along the deck, they found themselves on the bridge where the rest of the gang were standing huddled together, shivering in their oilskins. Huge waves broke over the ship in a creamy foam, carrying away anything which happened to be loose, and the cheerless gunmen — more used to warm flats and luxurious automobiles — cursed the weather and all its machinations with vehement fluency. Tiny Peters, an unlighted cigar between his thick lips, smiled sardonically as the helpless captives were dumped before him feet-first on the wet deck. His cruel eyes gleamed with evil satisfaction.

'So you thought you'd get the better of us, did you?' he snarled, making his voice audible above the clamour of the storm. He struck Michael across the face as a vicious emphasis to his words. 'You planned to bring the cops in and land us all in gaol, eh?' Then, as Michael made no reply: 'Well, Mr. Smarty, it seems as though something's misfired. The boot's on the other foot this time, and it's you who are going to pay, not us. You see, you both know too much, and that's bad. So we're sending you on a visit to Old Man Neptune.' He jerked his thumb significantly towards the boiling sea that raged below. 'He has a crush on folks who know too much.' He laughed raucously at his crude joke.

'You filthy swine!' exclaimed Michael. He struggled desperately, but the man who held him had him powerless. 'You can't get away with this, you know! You can't!'

Peters laughed.

'Can't we? We'll see about that in a minute,' he promised. He added, turning to Jill: 'Too bad of old Simon Shaw to bring his pretty niece into a business like this, wasn't it? He ought to have known how it'd end. It seems that the Shaw family's reducing pretty rapidly these days. Still, it can't be helped, can it?'

Jill's only reply was to close her eyes and sway unsteadily; then, before the man who was holding her had time to prevent it, she had crumpled to the deck and was laid in a heap at their feet. Michael panted as he strove to reach her.

'Leave her alone!' grunted Peters. 'She's only fainted, she'll be round in a minute; if she isn't, it doesn't matter!'

'You damned animal!' cried Michael. 'You can't kill a girl in cold blood. Blast you, Peters, it isn't human!' Then, much as it went against the grain to plead for anything: 'Look here, at least let her go. Do what you like with me, but for pity's sake leave her alone, can't you?'

Peters laughed — a harsh, humourless kind of a laugh.

'Quite the hero, aren't we?' he taunted. 'You poor fool! Do you think I'm so crazy? How long do you imagine we'd last in this racket if the girl went free? No, as I said before, she knows too much — and there's only one answer to that!'

'You fat, unspeakable slug!' hissed Michael. 'If I could only lay my hands on you — '

Peters sniggered and prodded Jill with his foot.

Her head moved and her eyes flickered, and Peters nodded.

'Lift her up, boys — she's coming round, I think.'

Michael watched her as she was hauled to her feet.

Her face was white and her eyes staring, but her lips were closed in a grim line of determination. She was terribly afraid and he knew it, but he had nothing but the deepest admiration for the way in which she was trying to conquer it. He knew that most would have struggled hysterically. But she . . .

'Ready?' The fat man looked at their captors enquiringly. 'All right, boys, you can dump 'em over.'

He raised his hand in a sardonic salute. 'Pleasant journey, both of you!'

They had a last glimpse of his grinning face, then the crooks were surging round them, and the next second they were standing shoulder to shoulder by the edge of the rail, with the raving wind plucking at their clothing and the driving spray whipping their faces. In that brief moment, Michael prayed as he had never prayed before. It was futile, he knew. No power in the universe could save them now . . . His eyes sought Jill's. She was smiling, and as he looked at her he felt a glow of pride that she could take it so pluckily. And then, for some obscure reason, a sickening pain surged through him at the thought of his leaving her — a girl whom he had known only a few brief hours. He felt suddenly that he should have known her before. Oh, if only . . . He saw her bloodless lips move; guessed rather than heard the words:

''Bye, Michael!'

He smiled back — or tried to. It was hard to smile in the face of death. Before, he wouldn't have flinched. But now . . .

It was at that moment when all hope seemed gone that help came. There was a sudden, awful crack, and a deep, even rumble that echoed even above the din of the storm. Peters looked upward as the ship lurched, and upon his features came a look of one who has seen his doom and is powerless to avert it. He pointed to the rain-lashed darkness above their heads, a choking, bubbling scream breaking from his throat. For an infinitesimal fraction of a second he gibbered meaninglessly, his shaking hands rising as if to ward off some frightful apparition. So much Michael saw . . . then what appeared to be several tons of hurtling rock swept relentlessly over the cowering crooks, and they disappeared forever from human vision. At that moment, something heavy struck Michael on the forehead. He had a hazy impression of being pressed forward over the rail. Then blackness over-whelmed him. He was unconscious long before his body struck the dark waters which reached up hungrily to engulf the cracking ship . . .

★ ★ ★

The captain of the tiny motor-yacht *Seasprite* shook the water from his oilskin as he paced the deck. It had been two hours since he had heard that strange and urgent message which had been picked up by the coastguard in his whitewashed hut high on the cliffs beyond Rockmouth, and he was beginning to think that his offer to put out to sea had been as much a waste of time as it had been ill-advised. For the search had been fruitless, and the best he could hope for now was to get back safely without piling up his ship on the rocky coast.

Suddenly he started, his hawk-like eyes sweeping the dark, rain-lashed sea. Was it his imagination, or did he see something out there to starboard? He muttered an excited exclamation and leaned over the rail. Then he leapt for the wheelhouse and, grabbing the engine-room telegraph, bellowed an order to stop the engines. The mate watched him in amazement.

'Sir — ' he began.

'Mr. Mate,' said the captain urgently, 'give orders to lower a boat. There's somebody out in that sea!'

The startled mate followed him as he rushed down the companion way to the lower deck, and because he knew the captain's word was law, roared an order for a boat . . .

'A boat, sir?' asked one of the seamen, unbelievingly. 'But a boat couldn't live in that sea!'

'Do as I tell you!' snarled the man; and a boat was lowered.

How much they had to fight to reach the tiny figure that was being tossed like a cork on the crest of the huge waves was known only to themselves. But reach it they did . . . and their astonishment when they found that it was a girl was unbounded. She was almost unconscious — but the inanimate figure of the young man she was supporting *was* unconscious!

8

The End of it All

'May — may I see him now?'

Jill put the question anxiously.

The nurse smiled. 'Yes, I think it will be all right.'

'Is he — ?'

'Quite safe.' The nurse nodded. 'I'm sure it was a near thing, though. If he hadn't such a marvellous constitution, I doubt whether he would have pulled through. Even then it would have been a losing fight if it hadn't been for you, Miss Shaw. If you hadn't been on hand at the crisis when he was calling for you . . . ' She smiled again; a slow, knowing smile. 'You saved his life. He's a nice, pleasant young fellow, Miss Shaw. He thinks a lot of you . . . '

'And I think a lot of him, too,' said Jill softly, as she slipped through the door into the tiny ward.

She moved quietly over to where Michael lay in bed, propped comfortably on a pile of pillows.

His eyes lit up miraculously as he saw her.

'Jill!' he exclaimed.

'Now, now, you mustn't get excited,' she remonstrated laughingly. 'The doctor says . . . '

'Blow the doctor!' he said, sitting up. 'I want to know about you.'

'Me?' She affected puzzlement. 'I don't know what you mean.'

'Oh yes, you do.' He looked at her straight in the eyes. 'You kept me afloat from a watery grave when I was knocked out, young lady. I want to thank you.'

'Oh, nonsense.'

'But you did, you know. You saved my life.'

'Don't be silly,' she protested. 'I only did what I could.'

'Did what you could? Ye gods, what a masterpiece of understatement. Why, if it hadn't been for you — '

'Nonsense,' she interrupted. 'If you hadn't saved my life earlier on, there would have been neither of us alive now.'

'What beats me is how you managed it at all,' he reflected. 'With your hands bound like that — '

'But didn't you know?' she asked him.

'Know what?'

'That I wasn't bound — at least, not properly. I'd been working on my ropes for ages — ever since I recovered consciousness, in fact — then, when I pretended to faint on the bridge — '

'*Pretended?* You mean you were spoofing? That you didn't faint after all?'

She smiled. 'Of course I didn't. I thought you'd guessed.'

'But why? Why did you do it at all?'

'So that I could gain another few minutes to get the ropes loosened altogether.'

'Well, I'll be — '

'I was scared stiff, of course. If they'd examined me — '

'Examined you? Why, after a faint like that, that was the last thing they'd do.' Michael stared at her, almost speechless with admiration.

Jill laughed.

'By the way,' he said suddenly, his brow darkening, 'what was it that — that came down and carried those poor devils away? I'm quite a bit hazy about that yet, and they've told me practically nothing . . . '

She shuddered.

'It was the cliff,' she answered. 'Somehow, the storm loosened it, and the whole lot went crashing into the sea. That was why the village was deserted, you know. It had been abandoned during the war because of undermined foundations and coast erosion. It wasn't safe. It caught quite a packet from the Nazis when they attacked our coastal defence batteries . . . ' She laughed ruefully. 'Funny, wasn't it, we never thought of a simple thing like that? Remember how inexplicable we thought it at the time? We ought to have guessed it was something like that. What confused me, of course, was coming on it so suddenly after we'd been so careful to follow the line. I was certain I'd never passed through a station like that before, and it never occurred to that we could have made a mistake and gone on to a branch-line in the fog . . .

'Anyway,' the girl finished, 'as I said before, it was the cliff. The ship must have drifted right under the most dangerous part of it, and . . . '

'Of course!' cried Michael, in sudden understanding. 'When we were in the wheelhouse, I made the captain give orders to up anchor, didn't I? When they got free, they must have forgotten all about it . . . Go on. What then?'

'Nothing then,' said Jill. 'It came right down on top of them and carried then to the bottom; that was all. Most of the village went too, incidentally. The inn and most of the houses on the front . . . The police think that Uncle Simon and the other two men who were left there . . . ' She broke off with a shudder.

'They were crooks,' he reminded her gently. 'Most of them were booked for the gallows, anyway.'

'Perhaps.' She nodded. She forced a smile. 'Anyway, that's all over now. I'm not sorry, either.'

They were silent, reflecting. Then Michael went on ruminatively: 'Come to think of it, you know, it was a pretty ingenious scheme. Using a deserted village on the coast to run illicit dope to England from the Continent. The place might have been made for them. Nobody ever went near — nobody ever had cause to — and even if they had, they wouldn't have found anything. It was one of the smartest games I've heard of for a long time — typical of Peters' dirty rackets — and they deserve credit for the idea, if nothing else . . . ' He broke off, frowning.

'What is it?'

'The only thing I don't understand is where your Uncle Simon comes into it.'

Her face clouded.

'That's the bit that's puzzling me,' she admitted. 'There's no doubt that he was mixed up in it, though nothing on earth will make me believe he was a willing accomplice.'

'No, I'm quite sure he wasn't. In fact, from what I overheard from the two men who were left in the village, I think it's pretty certain he was doing his best to get out of it. Apparently, that was why he was killed — to prevent him squealing. And that was why, when you turned up and introduced yourself as his niece, they thought he *had* squealed.'

'Poor Uncle Simon,' sighed Jill. 'Even now, I can hardly believe it. It's too dreadful to think about.'

'Then don't think about it at all,' he advised her. 'Put it out of your mind completely. It's all over now, and you can't alter the past. Which reminds me! Talking about the past — how long have I been here?'

'A week, almost.'

'A week? Good heavens! All that time? He was incredulous.

Jill laughed.

'You ought to think yourself lucky you're fit enough to talk, let alone grumble at how long you've been here.' Her voice softened. 'You've been ill, Michael — terribly ill. That bullet wound in your shoulder and those two bangs over the head didn't do you any good, you know, and you've been as near to contracting pneumonia as — '

'All right, all right,' he protested. 'I'll take your word for it.' He fell silent for a moment, his eyes distant. Then: 'You know, Jill, I've been thinking,' he said suddenly, 'and it strikes me that when I get out of this place I might want a bit of looking-after. Not medically, you under-stand, but — er — well, spiritually. You know: someone to keep an eye on me to see to it that I don't go falling out of any more trains. Mind you, it'd be a long job. I dare say it would take a lifetime. But — er — ' He hesitated. 'If I found that I did need someone like that . . . well, you don't think you'd care to take on the job, do you?'

Jill nodded. It was a breathless little nod.

'I think it's quite . . . possible,' she whispered.

THE STRANGER
AND THE INN

Rain. Splattering on windows, gurgling down drains, foaming into muddy torrents by the roadside. Rain and wind — a cold nor'wester which tore the brown leaves from the trees, howled derisively through keyholes, whooped in chimneys and banged doors. Grey scudding clouds, just skipping the tail of the weathercock on the church steeple. Dim daylight, fighting a losing battle against time and the elements; misty hills, huddled cottages, hurrying figures . . .

So night closed down on Little Frampton, and the storm raged unabated as it had done since the break of day. One by one, lights twinkled in the gloom, and from the dark crooked old inn at the end of the village street, there shone the warmest, cheeriest light of all — a deep ruddy glow which filtered through the drawn curtains like firelight through a glass of port wine.

It winked and beckoned and invited, and not even the fury of the storm could diminish its brightness, nor dissuade the habitués of the inn from finding their way from their own cosy firesides to the cosier hearth of the *Red Lion*.

Behind the curtains, in the snug parlour, a great fire blazed and crackled merrily; and a tall, white-faced grandfather clock gloomed solemnly out of its corner, measuring the minutes with a ponderous hand, and listening with approving wheezes to the general hum of conversation as the hours went by.

At nine o'clock precisely, when all the glasses had been refilled, all the pipes were alight to their owners' satisfaction, and fresh logs had been piled on the fire, the landlord, Mr. Tunstave, took his seat in the inglenook and looked sombrely around. The old clock thumped out its strokes with a great whirring and rattling; and, the place having become silent, Mr. Tunstave took a deep draught of his own excellent ale, and said:

'Gentlemen, you know that tonight is our special night, when we gather to tell stories of such spooky happenings as has been our lot to experience?'

There was a murmur of assent.

'And you know that story is always the same, being the creepiest thing that could ever happen to any living soul, and having the Hand of Providence in it?'

'Aye,' said the company, nodding as one man, and shivering slightly.

'I make no apology,' said Mr. Tunstave, 'for the repetition, for since that evening three years ago when it happened, our number has declined, and old faces have disappeared and new ones come — '

The fire roared, and trains of sparks went whirling up the chimney. A thousand tiny flames leaped and glimmered in the copper warming-pans on the wall, and in the brass fender, and in the depths of the tankards. The scream of the wind rose in pitch; the smoky oil-lamp flickered; a cold draught of air rushed through the room. A man stood in the doorway — a man dressed in a heavy motoring coat with the collar turned up, and a dripping trilby pulled over his eyes. He seemed to have materialised from nowhere, and he beckoned Mr. Tunstave to be seated as the landlord rose hurriedly to inquire his needs.

'I'm sorry if I interrupted you,' he said, and his voice was almost part of the wind in the chimney. 'Is this a private gathering? I found no-one in the public bar — '

'Well, sir,' said Mr. Tunstave, reluctantly, 'you wouldn't, not tonight. It's a kind o' special night, you see, and we 'ave a meeting in here and tell yarns — you know how it is.'

The Stranger nodded.

'What sort of yarns?' he asked. 'Are they private?'

Mr. Tunstave shook his head, and looked round at the staring, silent company.

'N-no, sir. O' course not. If you'd care to stay and listen, and join us in a drink — '

'Thank you,' said the Stranger, 'I'll have a drink shortly. Pray carry on, landlord, will you?'

'Very well, sir. But surely you'll take a seat — ?'

The man in the shadows waved his gauntleted hand in negation, and Mr. Tunstave, feeling ill at ease, blew smoke rings from his pipe and returned to his narrative.

'It was a night like this, gentleman — cold, rainy, and blowing a gale. (You remember it, John Cobb, for it blew down the lone oak at the end of your lane.) We was all sitting in here, round this self-same fire, talking about ghosts, when all of a sudden there comes a great crash from outside, as if a chimney-stack 'as fallen. I ups and opens the door, but it's dark and raining cats and dogs.' Here Mr. Tunstave cast a sidelong glance at the Stranger, but the man remained motionless and almost indistinguishable from the shadows, so the innkeeper continued:

'I was about to close the door again when I sees the searchlights out over in the direction of Marple Moor, and I 'ears the noise of engines up in the sky. Bombers, they was — our own lads coming back from Germany.' Mr. Tunstave shook his head reminiscently. 'I stands there and watches for a minute, and 'opes they're all returned safe. Then I comes back in, and says to Johnny Baker there, 'Johnny', I says, 'there ain't nothing to be seen except the searchlights,' and Johnny says, 'The old signboard's stopped squeaking, Amos, so I reckon that's what it was.' And I reckoned so too, for it was creaky and rusty, and almost on its last legs. And I says it's a good job none of us was underneath it.' A low mutter of agreement ran round. Mr. Tunstave held up his finger for silence, and a sudden great gust buffeted the window, and boomed fiendishly in the chimney, and above the noise of the storm, the grating creak of the inn sign came to their ears.

'Now here,' said Mr. Tunstave, 'comes the strangest part of the tale. I'd hardly crossed the room to sit down again when there comes a second crash, only this time it sounds as if the whole place is falling in. We jumps to our feet, properly alarmed, as you may suppose, and the door flies open and a man's standing there — almost where you're standing now, sir,' said Mr. Tunstave, addressing the Stranger. The man gave no sign of hearing. He remained silent and dark, his hands in his pockets and his face hidden. There was a mounting tension in the air; pipes went out unheeded and tankards of ale stood untouched on the tables. All eyes were fixed on the doorway.

'Before we could speak,' resumed Mr. Tunstave uneasily, 'the man flung out his arms and said, 'Go — go at once if you value your lives!' And his voice was like the wind among the tombstones in the churchyard.' He shivered at the memory. 'We were rooted to the spot with surprise, and were like to 'ave remained so if he'd not advanced a couple o' steps into the room and repeated his warning. We saw then a sight that made our 'air stand on end. He was dressed in leather flying clothes, with great gashes in 'is jacket, and 'is face was covered in blood. And 'orrors — we saw the old clock there clearly through his body!'

A half-burned log slipped down in the grate.

A tingle of fear stirred the hair of the listeners.

'We turned and fled,' said Mr. Tunstave

in a hushed voice. 'I don't mind admittin' it — we was scared to death. And two minutes later, a bomber crashed on the old *Red Lion* and demolished every stick and stone of it!'

Dead silence reigned after these words, as if the very storm itself were holding its breath. A timid little man in the corner said:

'You mean the ghost of the airman came to warn you of the crash before it happened?'

Mr. Tunstave was staring at the Stranger. 'Whether a man's ghost can appear to others while he's actually staring death in the face, I don't know,' he whispered, 'but I do know that's what happened that night — '

His voice was lost in a mighty squall which threatened to blow in the doors, and the screeching of the signboard outside was like that of a rusty file being drawn across a nail. Louder and more piercing it grew until — *crash!* — there was a snapping of tortured metal and a splintering of wood.

'My God!' exclaimed Mr. Tunstave in

horror. 'The sign's gone again!'

Transfixed, the occupants of the room watched the Stranger come slowly forward into the lamplight. Terror, stealthy and alive, gripped their limbs.

'Perhaps I can answer that question with one of my own,' he said in his odd, soughing voice. 'Can hosts make mistakes? You see, gentlemen, it was my aircraft which crashed that night, and I survived; but you — ' His voice was haunted and regretful. 'You died in the ruins of this inn. See — '

He took off his hat, and turned down the collar of his heavy coat. The assembled watchers saw his scarred, pitying face, and cried out in dread. There was a rumbling, earth-shaking roar; the storm rose to unbelievable fury. The lighted lamp, the fire, the clock, the glasses, the chairs and tables and the red curtains — aye, and the very occupants of the room — vanished, leaving the Stranger standing alone in the pouring rain, among dripping weeds and the lichened heaps of rubble that had once been the inn.

CORPSE IN THE
COTTAGE

1

Out of the Fog

The sign-post was useless.

Leaning drunkenly at an angle of seventy-five degrees, with one finger pointing earthwards and another two gesticulating towards heaven, its blackened and weather-worn hands registered nothing in the beam of the torch, and Paul Meredith cursed.

'Hell and damnation!' The imprecations which ran through his mind at that moment were juicy. For all the good it was, the beastly erection might never have been there at all. What the blazes was the County Council in these parts doing to neglect a thing like this?

Paul grunted and lowered his torch. The chill mist which had begun to rise with the coming of nightfall penetrated his jacket, and he shivered. Oh, well, there was nothing he could do here. He

131

trudged back to his car and slammed the door savagely as he climbed in before the wheel. Undecided, he glared through the windscreen into the thickening night. The two lanes in front of him which branched off into the darkness were narrow, dark and deserted. One of them, he knew, led into the village of Woodley; but the other, only heaven knew where! And as he expressively wished to arrive that night in Woodley — or at least in its near vicinity — the situation was disconcerting, to say the least of it.

His thumb sought the self-starter and pressed the engine into life again. Shrugging his shoulders, he turned the car down the nearest lane. After all, what was the good of trying to reason it out?

Of course, if he hadn't cleaned the car this morning and forgotten to replace the road-maps, this wouldn't have happened. Neither would it have happened if he hadn't had a puncture. Or even been allowed to start the journey earlier. But because Mrs. Smedley, his housekeeper, had insisted on his waiting while she loaded the rear of his car with what he considered to be enough bed-linen to supply an hotel — 'After all,' said Mrs. Smedley, 'you can't go and sleep in a cottage what's been empty for months on beds that won't be aired. Rheumatics, that's what you'll get!' — here he was crawling along the lanes of Surrey, miles from anywhere, with as much chance of arriving at Peter Stuart's cottage on the outskirts of Woodley as he had of taking wings.

Things, reflected Paul bitterly, were not going to plan. What sort of a plot could you evolve out of being lost in a dark country lane at — he glanced at the clock on the dashboard — half-past seven in the evening, when you were cold, hungry and tired?

There was nothing romantic about the tall, gloomy hedgerows which flashed by his car. Paul wondered whether there would be anything romantic about Peter Stuart's furnished cottage, either. Real author's haunt, Peter had declared enthusiastically. Far from the madding crowd and all that sort of thing. The very place for a popular novelist chap when he wanted to do some hard concentrating — so go and use it for as long as you like, old man. Go and use it.

Of course, Peter *would* insist on his having the key. And of course, Mrs. Smedley would arrange to have the place decorated from top to bottom. Just at the time when old Billy Handforth was demanding his long-overdue novel, and threatening to sue him if he did not turn it in within a month . . . So with luck like his, reflected Paul gloomily, the beastly place would turn out to be nothing more than a broken-down shack when he did get there. Old Peter usually exaggerated; and anyway, what sort of a dump could the place be with a name like 'The Larches'? He shuddered at the thought of it . . . and very nearly ran the portly form of Police Constable Herbert Feather into the ditch.

Paul jammed on his brakes as the blue-coated figure wobbled erratically across the glare of the headlamps to avoid him. He lowered the window as the car jerked to a standstill, and heard the officious grunts of the policeman as he dismounted his bicycle.

'What,' demanded Constable Feather in his best courtroom manner (Constable Feather could never forget that it had once been his pleasure to give evidence in a drunk-and-disorderly case at the Bishthorpe Petty Sessions), 'is the idea, young man?'

'Sorry, officer,' said Paul, groaning inwardly at the thought of a conflict with the local constabulary, 'I thought the lane was deserted,'

'Which is no cause for you drivin' on the wrong side of the road, an' dazzlin' people with headlamps like them. You very nearly killed me.'

Paul almost said he wished he had; but, realising that it was a remark which perhaps his victim would not appreciate, he proceeded to make amends instead.

'I'm very sorry,' he said, 'I'm afraid it was this mist that did it. As a matter of fact, I've lost my way, I'm *trying* to get to a village called Woodley. Am I anywhere near it?'

Mr. Feather melted under the amiable smile, and decided that perhaps his notebook had better remain where it was.

'Woodley? Yes, sir. You're on the right road, all right. Another couple of miles.'

'Thanks,' said Paul, smiling even more broadly. He was wondering whether it was worth it even for this. 'You don't happen to know of a place called The Larches, do you? It's somewhere on the outskirts, I believe; but which side, I don't know.'

'You're all right, sir,' said Constable Feather with equal geniality. 'It's just before you come into the village. On the bend at the left-'and side. You can't miss it.'

'Good,' said Paul. 'I'm very grateful to you, Constable.' He turned to the wheel again. 'I trust I didn't hurt you.'

'That's quite all right, sir. But I should drive a little slower if I were you. The mist's a bit thicker farther on.'

Paul promised he would, and before the constable had time to change his mind about issuing a summons, he had vanished down the lane.

The mist, as the policeman had predicted, did grow thicker along the road, and before long, Paul was reduced to little more than a crawl, with his eyes glued to the windscreen and his foot on the brake. He cursed the weather and all its machinations. The car bumped jerkily as it rattled over the rough stones of the country road. He'd travelled over two miles already. Of course, with his country-like exaggeration, the constable's two miles would probably turn out to be something like twenty . . . Then all at once the road turned, and as the headlights splashed over the dark leaves of the hedge, he had a brief glimpse of a wooden gateway.

The next second he had stopped the car and was switching off the headlamps. He reached for his torch and stepped out onto the roadway. The mist, damp and clammy, curled around him as he approached the gate. The two rusted hinges, dry and neglected, were almost in pieces; and the gate itself, half-open, was leaning precariously. Paul stopped and played the white beam of his torch over the woodwork. Dimly, beneath the dirt, he was just able to make out the words:

THE LARCHES

Paul sighed. Home at last — though by the look of things, perhaps it would be more comfortable to spend the night in the car.

Passing the gate, which wobbled perilously as he touched it, Paul made his way towards the house. Thick weeds choked the drive, giving his footfalls a muffled quality that did nothing to dispel the cheerlessness. Dimly, as he pierced the gloom, he could make out the dark bulk of the cottage ahead. 'Picturesque', Peter had called it. Ugh! Phantasmal was more like it!

Oh well, so long as there was a roof under which he could lay his head — and the abundance of bed-linen which Mrs. Smedley had thrust upon him — he didn't mind. For surely nothing else could happen now . . . ?

But even as he discredited the idea, something did happen. He was moving towards the porch of the cottage when suddenly he stopped. Slightly muffled by the blanket of fog, but still startlingly clear on the still night air, came the sound of a scream . . . then a moment later the door of the cottage burst open, and a dim figure came tearing towards him as if all the devils in hell were at its heels. There was no time to feel surprise; no time to swerve, even. For before Paul knew where he was, the figure had cannoned into him, and it was as much as he could do to keep his balance.

2

Visitors in the Night

In the first few moments of that strange encounter, Paul Meredith felt very much like the late Syd Walker, whose recurring misfortune had been to keep 'bumpin' into some queer how-d'yer-do' — why anyone should be screaming their head off in Peter Stuart's cottage at such a late hour as this, he couldn't imagine. The torch dropped from his fingers and clattered somewhere on the path. The next second the figure that had nearly knocked him over was in his arms, and a breathless voice was saying wildly:

'Let me go! I didn't see it! Oh, let me go!'

Paul jumped; so great was his surprise that he very nearly did let go. For the hot breaths which fanned his cheek and the tearful cries which accompanied them came unmistakably from a girl — and, by the sound of them, a young girl too.

'Steady on there!' said Paul, as she struggled madly in his grip. 'I want a look at you!'

'Oh, you brute!' cried the girl, desperately. 'Let me go, I tell you! Let me go!'

'Not yet, little lady,' gritted Paul. 'Ow!' This last remark was purely involuntary as the girl's teeth dug into his wrist.

Paul fumed. Girl or no girl, he wasn't going to have her take lumps out of him like that . . . and the manner in which he slapped her intimated as much.

From that moment, she capitulated. Her struggles ceased, and her trembling form became shaken by a paroxysm of sobs. Paul gripped her firmly by the wrist, and with his free hand stooped to recover the torch. Luckily, it was undamaged and still alight when he retrieved it, a bed of weeds having saved it from shattering.

'And now,' he remarked, 'we'll see who you are.'

He directed the beam on a small oval face which blinked at him in the sudden glare . . . then for a hushed moment the night and all its trials hung suspended

141

while he stared at her in breathless admiration. Never in his wildest dreams had he imagined anyone so bewitching; and Paul, whose labour it was to create heroines of every type, was a past master of the art. Young? Yes, she was young, all right. Hardly twenty, he considered. Though standing there with the torchlight playing garishly over her, her golden hair straying in delicious wisps over her smooth forehead, and her satin skin pale under the stress of her agitation, she looked little more than a schoolgirl.

Dazedly, he heard himself ask what she was doing here.

'Nothing!' she gasped. 'I shan't tell you! You can't make me tell you . . . ' She began struggling again.

'Can't I?' said Paul. And then, jerking himself out of his momentary stupor: 'But I can, you know. And I will if you don't hurry up and tell me voluntarily. What are you doing here at this time of night, and what made you scream?'

'Oh, you brute!' she exclaimed, struggling ineffectually in Paul's tightening grip. 'You know perfectly well what made me scream. If you're going to tell me that I imagined that body . . . '

Paul felt a sudden chill run down his spine.

'What body?' he echoed. He stared at her uncomprehendingly.

'The body in the cottage,' panted the girl. 'You know I couldn't miss seeing it. Let me go, I tell you! Let me . . . '

'Just a minute,' said Paul, becoming more than a little impatient. 'Do you mind telling me what you're burbling about? You sound like somebody out of a cheap thriller. What body?'

'Near the fireplace,' gasped the girl. 'I saw it . . . with blood all over its face.' She shuddered. 'You know it's there. You couldn't help seeing it.' She began weeping again. Paul shook her violently then drew her towards him.

'Look here,' he said. 'Stop that — stop it at once. I've never been to this place in my life before. I only arrived here a couple of minutes ago. Now — ' She choked back her sobs. ' — what are you trying to tell me? That there's a body in that cottage?'

She nodded.

'A dead body?' His tone was incredulous.

'Of course. I saw it.'

'Where?'

'I told you. Near the fireplace. In the sitting room. It — ' She closed her eyes. ' — it was horrible!'

'All right,' said Paul, releasing her wrist and gripping her by the arm instead. 'Show me.'

'No.' Her eyes opened wide again and filled with terror. 'Not back there. I won't!'

'Oh, yes, you will,' affirmed Paul, pulling her forward. 'And now, I don't know what little nightmare you've been having all on your own, but you're either going to prove it or disprove it. Come along.'

She gave a gasp, but that was all. Almost mechanically, it seemed, she allowed him to take her through the mist towards the cottage again, and before long they found themselves standing in the little hall. Paul flashed his torch over the panelled walls.

'Where?' he asked.

'In there.' Her voice was hardly more than a whisper as she pointed towards a half-open door which led off to the left. Paul took her by the arm again and directed her towards it, the white beam of his torch advancing before them.

It was more like a lounge, the place they entered, and one glance at the shadowy fittings told Paul that at least Peter did himself well, no matter how little he used the cottage. A second glance told him something further: that, however frightened was this girl, at least her story was true.

During the past few years, the number of corpses that had flitted their gruesome way through his novels had earned Paul the reputation of being aggressively realistic. It is strange to relate, therefore, that this was the first time he had actually encountered a body face to face, as it were . . . and at the moment he was hoping it would be the last.

Something inside him turned over as he crossed the room and gazed down at that horrible blood-stained face which leered up at him from the floor. He realised, too, how heartless he had been to bring the girl back to a scene like this.

He repressed a shudder as he turned away and moved back to the doorway.

'Well?' said the girl, with a touch of bitter sarcasm in her small voice. 'Do you believe me now?'

'Of course,' said Paul, speaking more civilly than he had done since he had met her. 'Do you know him?'

'I've never seen him before in my life,' she answered. Then, suddenly: 'Have you?'

'I told you. I only just arrived. So how could I?'

'Why? Don't you live here?'

'No.'

'Then how — ?'

'It belongs to a friend of mine,' explained Paul. 'He lent it me for a week or so, so that I could get a little work done. I was supposed to arrive earlier, but I got delayed, and — Here, wait a minute, he said suddenly. 'It's you who should be doing all the explaining, not I. Who are you, anyway, and where do you come from? And how did you get into the place?'

Just the faintest flicker of a smile touched her lips as she answered:

'The same way as we got in just now. Through the door. It was open.'

'Open?' said Paul. 'Who opened it?'

'I haven't the faintest idea,' she replied slowly. 'And to be quite candid, I don't particularly care. All I'm concerned with at the moment is putting as much distance between this place and myself as I possibly can. I've no fondness for corpses — particularly horribly mutilated ones.'

'Neither have I,' replied Paul. 'But I've a particular fondness for wanting to know what you're doing here. Suppose you explain.'

'Suppose you do,' she suggested.

'But I've already told you — '

'Have you? All right,' she agreed. 'Then we'll leave it at that, shall we?' And she made for the door.

Paul started.

'Here, wait a minute,' he said, pulling her back. 'Not so fast. You can't go off like that. I want an explanation.'

She shook her head.

'I've said all I'm going to say. And if you don't like it, you can lump it!'

Paul was indignant. He felt that the situation was running away with itself.

'You're pretty sure about all this, aren't you?' he snorted. 'You have the colossal cheek to break into my cottage — or what's virtually my cottage, anyway — find a dead body lying amongst the furniture, come flying out and nearly knock me into the middle of next week, and then expect to walk quietly away — leaving me to hold the baby!'

'And why not?' said the girl. By now she had recovered most of her composure, and was showing signs of possessing a will of her own. 'It's not my body!'

Paul's eyes gleamed. He said, tartly, 'It's certainly not mine, either!'

'All right, so what?'

'So I think it's up to you to tell me just what all this is about,' he said ominously.

The girl laughed. It was quite a pleasant laugh in its small, shaky way.

'Do you think I'm *quite* mad? If I

148

must, I'll say all I have to say before a policeman; but not to you. How do I know that you didn't do this?'

'Me?' Paul jumped; such a remote possibility had never even occurred to him. 'Here, I say — '

'Well, why not? You say this cottage belongs to a friend of yours, and that you've borrowed it for a week or two. How am I to know that you're telling the truth? How am I to know that you didn't kill him?' She shook her head. 'No, I'm not that kind of a fool. If you'll let go my arm, I'll walk quietly away and say nothing to no one. I dare say the police will get to know soon enough without my interfering. But if you won't — then I'm saying nothing till we've both seen a policeman!'

Paul looked at her for a moment, speechless. And then, at last:

'Well, of all the confounded nerve!' he exclaimed furiously. 'Damn it all, I don't even know your name, and yet you have the impudence to dictate to me like a blasted government official!'

She said, in a tired, impatient sort of voice:

'Well, do I go?'

'Damned if you do!' retorted Paul. 'At least, not until I know who you are and what all this is about.'

'You're not going to stand here all night?'

'I'm going to find out what you know about this business.'

She sighed. 'You're good at arguing, aren't you?'

'You're not so bad at it yourself,' he returned. 'Good heavens, woman! There's been a murder committed, and yet you stand here gibbering like a blasted monkey, and — '

He stopped abruptly, gripping her arm; and the hot retort which sprang to her lips was quelled. The torchlight faded and left them in darkness. She gave a tiny gasp and said: 'What the — ' But he squeezed her arm.

'Be quiet!' he whispered. 'There's somebody coming, I think.'

The girl listened as the pressure on her arm increased, and she realised for the first time that a car had pulled up outside the cottage. The dull throbbing of its engine came to her on the stillness, then suddenly died as it was shut down. There came the slam of a door and the babble of men's voices, than the crunch of footsteps on the weed-infested gravel. The diffused glimmer of torchlight showed faintly through the fog-bound window.

'Friends of yours?' she asked sardonically.

'Shut up!' The next second, he had dragged on her arm; and, having blundered their way across the darkened room, they were huddled uncomfortably behind the settee.

3

Dirty Work!

Crouching there, hardly daring to breathe, they heard the front door of the cottage creak as it was pushed further open, and a murmur of voices filled the hall.

Footsteps echoed on the parquet floor, and from their concealment they could just see bright flashes of torchlight stabbing the darkness.

A voice was saying hopefully:

'But maybe he's only unconscious. Maybe he isn't dead after all!'

'Don't be a fool, Stayner!' snapped another. 'Do you think I should have left him if I'd thought that? Of course he's dead. This way . . . '

A switch clicked. Light swamped the darkness in a dazzling flood, and both Paul and the girl blinked painfully in their hiding place behind the settee.

'There, see for yourself. He couldn't

possibly be alive with a wound like that!'

A sharp intake of breath sounded close to Paul's ear, and an impulsive movement came from the girl beside him. He glanced at her quickly, and saw a sudden gleam of recognition spring into her eyes.

He listened intently. The newcomers, clustered around the inert figure on the floor, were talking excitedly, and Paul would have given anything to know who they were. But his vision was limited to the flowered back of Peter Stuart's settee, and not for the world dared he risk a glimpse over the top.

'Yes, he's certainly had it!' a third voice was agreeing. 'Hell, boss, but we never reckoned for a killing, you know!'

'Do you think I did?' The other's voice was bitter. 'I tell you, I had to do it. When he thought that I'd found it, he simply went raving. I just had to hit him with the candlestick to defend myself. I never meant to kill him!'

'Well, whether you did or not, you've certainly done so!' commented the other. 'Anyway, what are we going to do with him? We can't leave him here. Besides, there's his car.'

'His car?'

'Yes, didn't you see it when we pulled up? No, maybe you didn't; the fog's pretty thick now . . . '

There was a startled exclamation.

'But that isn't his car. He never had one!'

'What's that?' The voice rose in alarm. 'Then who — ?'

'I don't know! You fool! Why didn't you tell me before! Maybe whoever it belongs to is in here now. If he is, we've got to find him. Come on!'

There was a hurried exit from the room. Voicing their speculations, the party began to make their way about the cottage. Paul grunted and came up from behind the settee like a very perplexed Jack-in-the-box,

'Well, well!' he murmured. 'Regular open house, isn't it? And who, might I ask, are those customers?'

'I don't know,' said the girl. She came up beside him warily.

'Sure?'

She looked at him quickly.

'Of course I'm sure. Why?'

'Oh, nothing. Maybe I only imagined that look of recognition in your pretty blue eyes. Never mind.' He moved away.

Sudden alarm seized her. 'Wait a minute. Where are you going?' she asked him.

'Me?' He stopped. 'Oh, nowhere special. Only to find out what the devil that bunch are up to. After that . . . '

She clutched his arm. 'You fool!' she hissed. 'You surely don't think you can tackle that crowd by yourself, do you? Don't be an idiot!'

He stared at her. 'Look here — ' he protested.

She went on hurriedly: 'You wouldn't stand an earthly at three to one. The best thing we can do is to get out of here as quickly as possible and find the nearest police station.'

'Well, of course, if you think I'm incapable . . . ' he began indignantly.

'I don't think anything,' she returned, brushing past him. 'Only for heaven's sake stop arguing, or you'll have us both caught. And keep that voice of yours down.'

'Well,' said Paul.

What strange quality there was about this girl, he did not know. All he did know was that it was something urgent — desperately urgent — he did not understand; but it was something that made him obey instantly. Watching her as she moved noiselessly across the room to stand listening at the door, he felt that by rights he ought to laugh; for, to his prosaic and disbelieving mind, she was behaving more like a character in a melodrama than a responsible person. But somehow he didn't. She was so deadly serious in all that she did that one simply couldn't laugh at her.

The heavy treads of the intruders came plainly from above as they searched the cottage. She whispered softly as he came up behind her:

'I think we're clear now. Come along.'

Almost mechanically, he followed her as she tip-toed into the hall. A wrought-iron lantern hung suspended from the blackened beams, throwing a feeble glimmer over the parquet floor, and seeming to make the fog-choked blackness of the night seem even denser as it eddied outside.

'Where to?' breathed Paul.

'Your car,' she said in an almost soundless whisper, moving towards the door. 'As quick as we can.'

In his mind, he heard himself counting as they crossed the hall: three . . . four . . . five . . . Another three steps, and they'd do it — and then —

'Move one inch, my dear Miss Marsden,' said a voice, cutting into his thoughts like the plunge of a rapier, 'and I'm afraid that will be the last movement you'll ever make!'

Simultaneously, they both swung round.

It was perhaps fully three seconds before Paul was able to realise what had happened; then, as he followed the girl's stricken gaze to the shadowy staircase, things were still not quite clear to him. But if he harboured any delusions as to their position, certainly the girl didn't, for she was like stone as she stared at the figure slowly descending the stairs.

It was the revolver that Paul saw first. As the man behind it came into the beam from the lantern, the gun muzzle gleamed dully, and Paul realised why the girl had stood so motionless. He realised something else, too, as that stocky, immaculately-dressed figure came more within range of his vision: that however broad and pleasant his smile might be, their antagonist was none the less formidable.

Paul stared at him as he came closer. He had a vague impression that others were coming down the staircase, too, but his attention was riveted on the man with the pistol. 'What a charming meeting, Miss Marsden,' he was saying in a smooth, mocking drawl, 'and how singularly fortunate. Sorry to detain you when you were so obviously on the point of leaving, my dear Jacqueline, but aren't you going to introduce me to this young friend of yours? I didn't know you numbered famous novelists like Mr. Paul Meredith amongst your acquaintances — for it is Mr. Meredith, isn't it?'

The girl started and looked at Paul in surprise. It jolted Paul, too.

'How the devil did you know that?' he demanded, and the man chuckled.

'Come, Mr. Meredith; when your books adorn every bookstall, and when you figure so prominently in the press, and when your photograph appears so consistently in the *Radio Times* . . . Oh yes, I've quite a memory for faces; and yours, I might add, is particularly familiar. In fact, in my more recreational moments, I'm quite a disciple of yours.' He went on: 'You'll forgive Miss Marsden's lack of etiquette, I know. I gather she's surprised to see me. And Miss Marsden is never at her best when she's surprised . . . And what, may I ask, brings a gentleman of your calling to a place like this, Mr. Meredith?'

Paul hesitated.

'I'm looking for local colour!' he replied at length, without the least intention of being humorous; and the man with the gun smiled.

'Witty,' he commented, 'quite witty. And how like your books, Mr. Meredith. So you're looking for local colour, are you?'

'All right,' said Jacqueline suddenly. 'You can cut all that stuff out, Ritchie.

Mr. Meredith, as you call him, has nothing whatever to do with this affair. In fact, I didn't know till now that his name *was* Meredith. So if you're planning any little unpleasantness by way of a reception, you'd better leave him out.'

'Leave him out?' echoed the man called Ritchie, in mock surprise. 'When Mr. Meredith is looking so hard for local colour? Come, my dear; you surely don't want to deprive one of the most promising young authors of the day of a little first-hand experience, do you? Why, you might even find yourself figuring in his next novel!'

'With you as villain, I suppose?' grunted Paul, with ugly vindictiveness born of an instinctive dislike of this smooth-tongued tailor's dummy.

'If you think I could portray the role — ' Ritchie smiled. ' — I should be honoured.' He gave a little bow. 'I think, my dear Jacqueline, you know quite well what I want,' he went on, and suddenly his voice had become so low and concentrated that Paul almost shivered.

'And if I haven't got it?'

'Oh, but my dear Jacqueline, I'm quite

sure that you have got it,' said Ritchie. 'So denying it would be quite useless, wouldn't it?' He waited a moment, watching her, then: 'Well, are you going to be sensible?'

Jacqueline hesitated. She cast a sharp glance towards Paul, who was watching her dazedly. After all, she reflected, it wasn't what one could call an orthodox situation, even for an author. In fact, she realised that to Paul the affair must seem more like something out of a nightmare. And when one becomes irrevocably entangled in another's nightmare . . .

She turned to Ritchie again.

'You won't believe me,' she said scathingly, 'because it isn't in you to believe anything. But I've been in this cottage for less than ten minutes, and I've no more idea where it is than you have.'

'And your boyfriend?' The other's tone was like ice.

'He isn't my boyfriend,' said Jacqueline, 'and I've never seen him before in my life.'

Ritchie sighed. There was no doubt as to how much he credited this information.

'My dear Jacqueline,' he said wearily, 'I really thought you'd know better. However, if you will persist in being awkward . . .You realise, of course, that I've no intention of leaving this cottage empty-handed?' He sighed again. 'Well, if you must . . . ' He gave a quick signal with his hand.

Without a word, the other two who were standing around then closed in on her. Jacqueline backed away instinctively. Sudden fear welled in her eyes. She knew Ritchie — knew him well.

'Take her into the kitchen,' said Ritchie coldly. 'She'll talk, all right!'

Jacqueline struggled. A coarse hand choked back the cry which sprang to her lips. Her frantic eyes caught those of Paul, then she was being whipped through to the rear of the cottage.

Paul awoke from his daze.

'Wait a minute,' he said, thrusting himself forward. 'I don't know what the devil you're trying to do, but if you so much as touch a hair of that girl's head, I'll . . . '

'Yes, Mr. Meredith?' sneered Ritchie, bringing the barrel of his pistol between them. 'You'll what?'

Paul halted as the barrel of the pistol dug into his side. He saw the creamy fingers of the man called Ritchie curl tentatively around the trigger. And then he looked upwards and saw the smooth, grinning face.

And at that moment Jacqueline screamed.

That did it. From the very first moment of that eventful day when Mrs. Smedley had insisted on his staying behind while she fussed with the bed-linen, everything had gone wrong. Straw upon straw of irritation had been piled upon him relentlessly. And now, indeed, this was the last. The back of the camel was not only broken, he felt, but positively shattered into a thousand pieces.

He lunged at Ritchie, heedless of the revolver. It didn't occur to him that it was suicidal. In fact, there was very little that did occur to him during those few hectic moments. There was a startled shout and a scuffle of feet. There was a curse from Ritchie. Then, in an undignified moment, Paul felt himself in close contact with the parquet floor; and before he had time to rise to the perpendicular to resume his attack, he felt an unfriendly wallop on the side of his head, and from that moment his temper and everything else fled. The struggle was over.

4

Torture Stuff!

Paul Meredith slid slowly back to consciousness. There was never any dividing line between sleep and wakefulness: one moment he was in the depths of blackness, and the next he was vivid and alert.

He was acutely aware of a throbbing pain which claimed his head, and with the realization of what had caused it, came the realization of other things too.

Had not the memory of Jacqueline's last scream been implanted so firmly within him, Paul would have been inclined to believe that he was just recovering from one of Peter Stuart's celebrated binges, and that the firework display which flamed before his eyes — open or closed — was just another hangover, slightly heavier than the last.

But no hangover, however outsized,

could account for a cry like that; and with the horror of it still ringing in his ears, he looked around him.

He was back once more in the sitting room of the cottage, and the light was still on. But whereas before everything had been a picture of unlived-in tidiness, everything was now chaos. The carpet was turned aside; one or two loose floorboards were ripped up; drawers were pulled out, their multifarious contents strewn everywhere; books from the bookcases were scattered indiscriminately; even the pictures from the walls had been taken down. In short, the room had been ransacked from top to bottom.

The toes of a pair of shoes sticking out from behind the settee caught his gaze, and he realized with an unpleasant shock that he was in company with the corpse. He started towards it involuntarily, then realised all at once that he couldn't; that he was bound and foot to the chair on which he was sitting. He smiled grimly. How classic!

A soft intake of breath sounded somewhere near him, and he turned his head sharply — and nearly toppled backwards in his chair in surprise.

'Miss Marsden!' he gasped. 'Thank heaven you're all right. I was afraid that greasy blighter . . . '

Jacqueline smiled at him a trifle wanly. He was sitting bolt upright in a chair a few feet away, similarly bound.

'I'm afraid I fainted,' she said, 'so there was nothing much they could do — except leave me like this while they pulled the place to pieces.'

Then, with obvious relief, 'I thought you were never going to come round. I was afraid Ritchie had hit you just a little too hard. Still . . . ' She stopped, suddenly, worriedly, then hurried on: 'Look, I'm sorry for dragging you into an affair like this. I'd have given anything in the world to have been able to save you from it all, but . . . '

'Sorry, be damned!' said Paul, briskly. He slewed his chair round so that he could address her more directly. 'Wait till I get my hands on that walking barrel of lard, that's all!'

She frowned.

'I'm afraid you might not get the chance,' she said quietly. 'Ritchie isn't quite the fool he looks, and he really can be quite unpleasant when the situation arises.'

'And will it arise?' He looked at her quizzically.

'It's arisen already. Unless I tell him where to find what he wants, he's liable to turn nasty.'

'But you won't tell him, will you?' said Paul, his eyes glinting.

'It's not only that I won't, but that I can't,' she replied. 'I don't know where it is — honestly . . . oh, if only Daddy had known what he was after in the first place . . . '

'Then it isn't his? What he's after, I mean? Wait a minute,' said Paul. 'Who is your father, anyway? I'm all in the dark about this. Hadn't you better begin at the beginning, so that I can get a proper slant on things?'

She smiled at him wistfully.

'I'm sorry things have been so confusing to you; it must have been horrid. Yes, I suppose I'd better before they come back.'

There was a terrific bump from the room above them, and a shower of plaster came raining upon them. Paul glanced upwards.

'If they go on like that, they'll be back sooner than they intend! Go on.'

'You remember my father, don't you?'

He nodded. 'I think I do, now that I know your name is Marsden. He had something to do with the discovery of a new aviation spirit, hadn't he? I believe the papers made quite a fuss of it at the time.'

'That's right. He'd been working on the idea for years, though I hardly believe he ever expected to perfect it. However, he *did* perfect it, and his discovery was worth millions.

'I don't know whether you realise it, but up to now the chief drawback to long-distance flying has been the enormous amount of fuel required for the journey. No aircraft has been designed that has been able to carry anything near the amount, and the only alternative has been to split the journey into stages, refuelling at the end of each stage.'

'But your father discovered something better, eh?'

'Infinitely,' said Jacqueline. 'Daddy's new spirit cut fuel consumption by a quarter, which meant that it was possible to take the longest distance in a single hop. It revolutionised the aeronautical world completely.'

'Which is where our friend Ritchie comes in, I suppose?'

Jacqueline nodded.

'Ritchie's a research chemist. Up till two years ago, Daddy and he carried out experiments jointly, but with no results. Then Ritchie quarrelled, and the partnership broke up. Now he's claiming that Daddy's discovery is really his, and that Daddy had nothing whatsoever to do with it.'

'Surely it shouldn't be very hard to refute the claim?'

'That's just the point,' said Jacqueline. 'It wouldn't be difficult at all — if I could find the formula!'

Paul's eyebrows shot up.

'You mean it's missing?'

Jacqueline nodded.

'And you're looking for it . . . here? Pardon me if I'm a bit sceptical, but Peter Stuart's cottage is just about the last place in the world I should think of for looking for a missing formula. You wouldn't like to explain?'

'It was just before Daddy died,' she said. 'He hadn't been well for a long time, and I believe he had some sort of premonition that somebody was after it, although he never told me a thing, for he took it about with him wherever he went. He'd been up to the Air Ministry to discuss the matter with some Air Ministry officials, and he was on his way home. The car broke down, so he got out and went for a stroll along the road while the chauffeur attended to it. When the chauffeur found him some time later, he — he'd been attacked.' Her voice faltered. 'He died as a result as a result of the assault, two days later.'

'Yes, but — '

'When we came to examine his papers, the formula had gone. Yet he'd had it during that visit to London; he'd had it when he left the Air Ministry.'

'Stolen?'

She shook her head.

'That's what we thought, of course. But when Ritchie turned up demanding the formula, we knew that it couldn't have been him, at any rate. So the only conclusion we could come to was that Daddy had hidden it.'

'And you thought — ?'

'Not until recently. Not until I happened to be driving past this place a few days ago and saw the name on the gate. Then I realised that what Daddy had been saying before he died had not been mere gibberish, delirium — that his repeated references to 'larches' could have only one meaning. Don't you see? Where else could he have hidden it? His car broke down not many yards from this spot; there was nowhere else.'

Paul nodded.

'Now I'm beginning to see daylight,' he said, 'but only partially. If your father had already been in touch with the Air Ministry people about this new invention of his, what use is the formula going to be to Ritchie when he does find it?'

Jacqueline laughed.

'Britain isn't the only country who does long-distance flying, you know. Just about every country in Europe and elsewhere would give anything to gain possession of the formula. And anyone having it to sell, could make a fortune.'

'Yes of course,' agreed Paul. 'But what about our friend behind the settee? Where does he fit into the picture?'

'Oh, that's Grantham,' replied Jacqueline, and Paul stared.

'Grantham? Do you mean you know him? But I thought you said — '

'Oh, I said lots of things. But that was because I didn't know you. Poor Grantham. That was why I was so scared when I saw him — I'd no idea he was after the formula also. He used to be Daddy's chauffeur.'

'I see. So there was a couple after it, eh? But, I say, how did they know the formula, was likely to be here in the first place?'

'Oh, that's easy,' said Jacqueline. But that was as far as she got. For at that moment footsteps sounded on the staircase, and Paul hissed quickly:

'Now for it!'

'Well, well, Miss Marsden,' purred Ritchie as he entered the room. He smiled sweetly. 'Quite a nice little tête-à-tête, eh? So glad Mr. Meredith has recovered sufficiently to entertain you. Feeling better, Mr. Meredith?'

'Go to hell!' snapped Paul politely, and Ritchie laughed.

'Really,' Mr. Meredith,' he drawled mockingly. 'What a nasty temper that is. And for a man in your position, too. What *would* your public think of you . . . ? Still, perhaps there's some excuse. Having one's exuberance restrained by the butt of a revolver, then being tied to a chair . . . not really soothing, is it?'

'Blast you!' said Paul. There was a dangerous glint in his eyes. 'Why, you overfed tailor's dummy, for two pins I'd — '

Ritchie nodded.

'I've no doubt you would,' he agreed, 'if you were in a position to do so. So it's just as well that you're not, isn't it, Mr. Meredith? Besides, there's been enough violence for one night — and I loathe violence.'

Paul's eyes strayed to the figure behind

the settee. He said pointedly, flashing a glance at Ritchie:

'Do you loathe murder also?'

'Particularly murder, agreed Ritchie, 'though I'm not prepared to stop even at that little pleasantry to gain, my purpose. So you see, Mr. Meredith, I'm not a man to be trifled with, am I?'

Paul glowered.

'However,' went on Ritchie, unperturbed, 'if nothing else, I am considerate, and I like this painful situation no more than you do. So what about bringing it to an end for all of us by telling me what I want to know? Just tell me where I can find this tiresome formula, and we'll have things settled in no time.' He paused. 'Well, Mr. Meredith?'

Paul looked at him.

'I don't know what the devil you're talking about!' he snapped. 'Miss Marsden has told you that already.'

Ritchie sighed. There was a world of tolerance in that sigh.

'Then maybe Miss Marsden can help us?'

'You know quite well that I can't,' said

Jacqueline promptly. 'Even if I wanted to. I've no more idea than the man in the moon where it is. And as for Mr. Meredith — '

'Yes, Miss Marsden?'

'As for Mr. Meredith, I've already told you that he knows less about it than I do.'

'Oh, come, my dear,' said Ritchie. He was vaguely disapproving. 'This isn't being sensible, you know, not sensible at all.'

'But I've already told you — '

'That your father died without whispering so much as a syllable,' he finished. 'Yes, I know. But surely you don't expect me to believe that, do you?'

'I should think you'd find it difficult to believe anything!' grunted Paul. Then, impatiently: 'Damn you man, can't you see when she's telling the truth?'

'Oh yes, I'm sure I can,' replied Ritchie. Then all it once his demeanour changed, and his voice became hard and concentrated. 'At the moment she's not telling the truth; nor are you. But you're not going to fool me, Mr. Meredith — either of you. You didn't come down here just to look at the scenery. You came down to get the formula, didn't you?

'Formula, my foot!' exclaimed Paul disgustedly. And then, with anger: 'Damn the formula! Blast the formula! I didn't even know that there was such a thing until a short while ago, and I certainly didn't come down here to look for it! I came down here to be quiet and to do a bit of writing — you've only to look in the back of my car at my typewriter and things to prove that — but instead it seems that I've walked into a madhouse! And if you can't believe that, then be hanged to you.'

Ritchie was unmoved.

'No, Mr. Meredith,' he went on, 'you didn't come down here just to look at the scenery. You came down to get the formula. Well, you're not going to get it — I am. And you're going to help me.'

He looked at his wristwatch.

'I'm going to give you just two minutes to make up your minds. If, by that time, you haven't done so, I shall endeavour to help you. And I assure you,' he added unpleasantly, 'that neither of you will like my assistance one little bit!'

His hand went to his breast pocket as he finished, and he pulled out a gold cigarette case. Quite slowly, he extracted a cigarette and tapped it on the outside. Then, placing it to his lips, he snapped on a lighter and drew deeply. He exhaled a thin stream of grey smoke as he pocketed the lighter.

There was a silence. So utter that Paul could almost hear the thumping of his own heart. His gaze sought Jacqueline's across the room. There was an expression in her eyes he could not read; he thought it was something between fear and determination. He saw, too, that she had gone pale; but what she was thinking, he did not know. He looked round at the others, and for the first time he saw what they were really like. Unsavoury customers, all of them, from Ritchie downwards.

It was Ritchie's voice that brought him to earth again.

'Well, Mr. Meredith; have you decided?'

Paul's expression showed plainly that he had not decided anything. Ritchie shrugged and turned to Jacqueline again.

'What about you, Miss Marsden? Are you going to be sensible?'

Jacqueline choked.

'Ritchie, I can't tell you,' she insisted. 'I don't know.'

The other snapped his fingers impatiently. It was like the signal for an execution . . .

'Untie her!' he ordered crisply. 'But keep her in the chair . . . That's right.' He nodded in approval as the bonds fell from her. 'I hope it won't be necessary to go beyond the first stage of this operation, my dear, but in case it is . . . I told you I should give you both two minutes, didn't I? Well, your two minutes are up.' He drew hard on his cigarette. 'I dislike ill-treating my fellow-creatures intensely, especially when they happen to be young ladies, but unless one of you changes your mind here and now, I am afraid it will be my unpleasant duty to burn a hole in Miss Marsden's pretty cheek with this cigarette. And I should hate that.'

Paul started.

'You wouldn't dare! Blast you, you wouldn't dare!'

'Miss Marsden knows whether or not I'd dare — don't you, Miss Marsden?'

It was obvious that the girl knew only too well . . . Ritchie moved to the back of her chair and leaned over her. She looked up at him.

'Ritchie, I can't. I don't know. I swear I don't know . . . '

'No?' Ritchie's thick lips smiled humourlessly. 'Think again, my dear. Think again . . . '

Paul tugged hard at his bonds, but it was of no avail. He was powerless. He pulled his gaze away with an effort and cast his eyes about him wildly.

There was no mercy in Ritchie; he could see that.

And unless he could do something, and do it quickly . . . He shuddered at the alternative.

'Well, my dear?'

'Ritchie,' choked Jacqueline. 'You've got to believe me! You've got to . . . '

She felt the warmth of the cigarette as it neared her cheek, and the words stuck in her throat.

The smoke of it got into her nose and

tingled her eyes as it wafted past her. She could hear Ritchie's laboured breathing close to her ear, and she knew that it was no use appealing. She thought desperately of springing to her feet and making a break for it, but the sight of one of Ritchie's confederates standing before her, pistol in hand, quelled any hopes she might have in that direction. She closed her eyes, tensed and waited for the pain she knew must come, and she waited . . . waited . . .

Till she realised all at once that there was no pain. That Ritchie was bending over her no longer.

And that someone was knocking thunderously on the door!

5

The Other Foot

Ritchie sprang into the middle of the room with a muttered oath. For a split second he stood motionless, his face grey. Then the knocking came again, louder and more insistent.

'Quickly!' he said to the man near him. 'Quick! Stayner, you fool! Don't gape. See who it is!'

As Stayner crossed to the door, the man with the gun moved nearer, covering them threateningly, his finger tightening on the trigger. In the tense silence that followed, they heard Stayner's footsteps as he crossed the hall, and the rattle of the latch as he opened the door. And then, muffled as if by the mist, an apologetic voice came wavering from the doorstep.

'Evenin', sir.' Paul could almost visualise the owner as he saluted deferentially. 'Sorry to bother you, sir, but it's about them cars. You'll 'ave to move 'em, you know, else there'll be an accident. Right on the corner, they are, an' the mist's gettin' thicker every minute.'

Paul almost laughed. It was the constable — he would have known that voice anywhere! The rustic arm of the law whose rural life he had so nearly terminated on his way down here. And at the crucial moment, too.

But the man with the gun was quicker, and any hopes Paul had entertained in that direction were dashed. Even as he opened his lips to call out, the other darted forward and clamped a large hand over his mouth, and the cry was choked before it was uttered. Paul jerked his head in an effort to evade the hand, but it was no use. His eyes blazed. Panting heavily, he kicked out at the gunman, and as the hand broke away from his mouth, Paul felt his chair go toppling backwards towards the fireplace.

There was a splintering of wood as the chair collapsed under the strain, and the next moment his head came in contact with the fender, and partial blackness descended upon him.

Ritchie, muffling Jacqueline by a similar method, glanced anxiously at the fallen figure, but Paul was too dazed to raise the alarm now.

'Sorry, Constable,' came back from the hall. 'We were having a little — er — party, and we didn't realise. But we're going in a minute, so you needn't worry . . .'

'Maybe so, sir,' replied the policeman, tolerantly, 'but that won't do, sir, and I'll 'ave to ask you to shift 'em now. Proper dangerous, they are.'

'Yes, but —'

'Sorry, sir!' It seemed that the constable was inclined to be obstinate in his officialdom. 'But duty's duty, an' if you *don't mind* . . .'

What dire consequences would be the alternative, he did not say. He merely broke off suggestively.

'All right! If you'll just wait a minute till I get somebody else . . .'

There was no help for it, inconvenient as it might be to everyone else. It seemed that Police Constable Herbert Feather had made up his mind to see those cars safely removed, and until he had done so he was likely to prove awkward.

Ritchie swore and fumbled in his pocket for a handkerchief. A few seconds later it was around Jacqueline's mouth — a temporary but efficient gag. 'Blast!' grunted their captor. 'Local bumpkin! If we're not careful, there's no telling what he might see. Keep them covered, Shand, and make sure they don't make a sound; we'll only be gone a couple of minutes.' He moved to the door.

'All right, Constable. We'll shift the cars for you. If you'll have a little patience . . .'

And the three of them want tramping down the drive through the fog . . .

Shand moved to the fireplace and kicked the broken chair from under his prisoner.

'Up you get, hero!' he drawled. 'Too bad your little plan came unstuck!'

Paul, shaking his head to clear his thoughts, staggered to his feet, stripping the loose rope from his hands as he did so. The hard shape of Stayner's revolver dug into his back, prodding him across the room.

'You heard what he said,' he grunted. 'One squeal, and it'll be your last; play possum, and you'll be all right. And just so as we're all nice and comfy, let's have you both on the settee where I can keep an eye on you. Come on . . . '

Paul shot a quick glance around him, his thoughts racing. Only one man now stood between them and their freedom. True, there was also a revolver to be reckoned with, but before many seconds the others would have returned, and the odds would be even more overwhelming. If he could get out of the range of that revolver for a second . . . If only . . .

He shrugged.

'All right,' he said truculently. 'But you might go easy with that fire-iron — I'm not such a hero as all that, and those are my ribs you're denting!'

Shand prodded him relentlessly across the room.

'Skip it, mister. Sit down and look pretty. And keep still.'

Paul did sit down. But he didn't keep still. Resignedly, he flopped back against the cushions . . . and brought his feet up from the floor in a terrific kick. This time he was more successful.

It was timed perfectly.

A stout pair of number nines sank joyously into the pit of Shand's stomach, and there was a puncture-like gasp. Shand folded like a penknife.

Jacqueline watched dazedly. 'That's number one account, sweet one!' observed Paul, lightly. 'Number two coming right over . . . '

It was. It all happened so swiftly that Shand had no time even to regain his breath. In a commando-like tackle, Paul bounded from the settee and landed squarely on top of him . . . and the revolver went skidding across the floor.

From that moment, all was confusion.

Shand's first impression was that the sun, the moon and the whole universe had fallen to pieces on top of him. His second was that a hefty and vicious mallet was trying its hardest to dislocate his jaw. It took him just two seconds to realise the truth . . . then Paul's fist came down for the final reckoning, and he knew no more.

'Well, well!' muttered Paul, as the figure

beneath him lay suddenly still. It was a most complete and final stillness. 'There's something to be said for this Up in The Morning business after all!'

As he came to his feet, he found Jacqueline beside him, the gag torn from her mouth,

'Oh my god!' she gasped in a hushed little whisper, vibrant with fear and relief. 'Is he really . . . unconscious?'

'Sleeping like a baby.' Paul nodded with satisfaction, licking his knuckles. 'And likely to for some time to come. Now, where's that revolver?' He moved across the room and retrieved the weapon from a corner. 'There, that's better,' he said, weighing it in his hand, 'we're more evenly balanced now. Do you think you can find something to tie him up with to keep him out of harm's way? Right now, I've another account to settle . . . and I'm settling it straight away!'

And he had gone before she had time to answer him.

Outside, the fog met him like an inky curtain. He pulled up on the doorstep and strained his eyes.

The damp chill of the night air came down upon him like a cold douche after the excitement of the past few minutes. Cold sobriety changed places with warm impulsiveness. No use for high-pressure stuff here, he decided. Sound common sense and levelheadedness were what was needed.

He peered through the blackness.

Somewhere in the distance a feeble glow in the whirling mist marked the position of the cars. An engine throbbed dully. He thought back for a moment. What was it Peter had said? 'Doll's house of a garage by the side of the cottage . . . but if you don't want to bother, there's a drive leading up to it big enough to park upon' . . . Paul nodded to himself. Of course — the drive branched off to the right, didn't it? So, to keep the constable quiet, it was obvious they'd park the cars there.

He set off down the drive, clutching the revolver tightly. He trod lightly over the gravel and weeds, noiseless, melting into the fog until he became almost a part of it. The essential thing now was surprise;

his attack on the unfortunate Shand had been so swift and soundless that they couldn't possibly have heard it.

He heard the revving of an engine, and saw a diffusion of light grow brighter as the car swung towards him. He recognised the purr of the engine instantly: it was his own. He halted beside a clump of bushes and drew into the shadows of them.

The light passed him and faded into the mist again, becoming stationary as the car drew to a standstill before the door of the garage. The white haze of diffraction spread through the fog. He heard the clash of a door, then Ritchie's voice said:

'All right, Stayner. You can come in now.'

There was another bright glare as the car swung round, the crunch of gravel and a squeal of brakes. Then an uncanny silence descended as the engine was cut off. A light faded and a door slammed.

'There we are, sir,' came a ponderous voice which Paul identified as that of Police Constable Feather. 'Didn't take a minute, did it? An' much safer for everybody.'

Ritchie mumbled something that Paul couldn't hear, and the constable coughed.

'That's all right, sir. Duty's duty, as I said, an' there's enough accidents on the roads today without askin' for more . . . Thank you, sir; that's very 'andsome of you. Now I'll leave you to get on with your party. Goodnight, sir . . . an' thank you!'

Paul gripped the revolver tightly as the policeman began to move away. He felt that the time was now, for with a representative of the law on the scene . . . He saw the dim shapes of the two men come together and move towards the house. He heard Stayner whisper something uncomplimentary about the constable. And then, with his trust in the gods and his mind eager and alert, Paul detached himself from the clinging embrace of the bushes and planted himself firmly in the path of the oncoming couple.

6

Postcard from Peter

Ritchie's first intimation of impending danger was a sudden jar as his stocky figure collided violently with the unseen form in the darkness, and a circle of steel prodded him ominously in the stomach. For perhaps a full moment the unexpectedness of the encounter unnerved him. Then, as Paul's voice hissed menacingly in his ear, his wits returned, and he had weighed up the situation in a flash.

'Don't move!' rasped Paul, as they both backed away instinctively. His revolver raked them in the darkness. 'I warn you, I'll shoot!'

'Hell!' gasped Stayner. Incredulity muffled his voice to a hoarse croak, and stunned him into submission. 'It's Meredith. How the hell — '

He broke off with a jerk as Ritchie brushed past him in an attempt to escape into the dark. But Paul was quicker. A strong hand shot out, and Ritchie's arm was hooked in a grip of iron. A ripple of laughter broke the stillness.

'Not this time, Boy Blue,' admonished Paul. 'I want you inside . . . Constable!' He raised his voice. 'Hey there, Constable!'

'You fool!' spat Ritchie. Cold anger burned in his voice and his eyes flashed. 'Let me go, blast you! Let me go, I tell you! You'll have that blithering policeman down on us . . . '

'That, my dear sewer-rat,' said Paul sweetly, 'is the idea precisely; not that I expect you to appreciate it. Ah, ah!' He tightened his grip. 'I've warned you!'

The dull glow of the constable's lamp halted abruptly as Paul's voice cut through the woolly stillness. There was a moment of hesitation, then a muffled Constable Feather enquired:

''Ello, there! Anythin' wrong? Did you shout, sir?'

'Yes, you idiot!' yelled Paul, a trifle unkindly. 'This way. Hurry up, man!'

There was a crunching of gravel and a

bobbing of light as the constable hurried towards the house again. Ritchie swore and wrenched furiously in Paul's grip.

'Stayner, you half-wit! For heaven's sake, do something!' he hissed. 'His revolver — quick!'

Stayner started and jerked himself together. He dived frantically for Paul's fingers, but the young novelist dodged him in a neat sidestep, dragging his captor with him. It was only a temporary reprieve. The next second, Stayner was on him again. In the choking mist, it was like grappling with a nightmare. Despite his efforts, Paul felt his weapon arm being forced downwards, and desperately he snatched at the trigger. But his chance had passed. There was a spurt of flame and a crack that rang loudly in their ears, and the gravel from the drive came splintering around them. Then a burning pain stabbed Paul's arm as it was twisted behind him, and a sharp cry broke involuntarily from his lips. There was only one answer to that. Releasing his hold on Ritchie, he brought his left arm round with terrific force into the face of his adversary.

Bone met bone as a pile-drive punch — brother to the one that that had knocked out Shand — found its mark, and Stayner gave a groan as he measured his length on the drive and stayed there.

It was Ritchie's chance, and he took it. Quick as lightning, he turned to flee . . . and dashed straight into a sudden bright glare that almost dazzled him.

Police Constable Feather gasped as he staggered under the impact.

''Ere, wait a minute,' he began indignantly. 'Dashin' about like an 'erd of elephants an' knockin' folk over! What . . . '

'Get out of the way, you idiot!' snarled Ritchie as he shook off the policeman's encumbrance, and the constable bridled.

'Now, look 'ere. What I say is — ow!'

A mighty push that neatly deposited him on the drive put an end to the policeman's bombastic objections, and Ritchie sped past him into the night.

'Blast!' groaned Paul in bitter disappointment. 'You've let him go, damn you! You've let him go!'

The dense fog closed around Ritchie in a clammy mantle, and he vanished from sight. His heart thumped and his eyes glittered, and for once the imperturbability that was his pose was shattered. Somewhere behind him, he could hear Paul's footsteps in dogged pursuit, and he cursed. Damn the man!

If it had not been for him ... How things had gone wrong, he could not imagine; but that Paul was to blame, Ritchie had no doubt. He remembered Stayner. Weaponless — for the revolver was now in Paul's hands — there seemed to be only one thing for it. To clear out while the going was good; and to clear out quickly!

The grey vapour choked him as he ran blindly, swirling round him like a blanket that grew darker and darker as he fled farther from the house. His racing feet stumbled over gravel and weeds, but where he was, he had no idea. He kept hearing Paul's voice, and the patter of footsteps sounded alarmingly near. Desperately, he strained every muscle.

Then all at once his flight was checked. A mighty crash that shook every bone in his body sent him staggering and wrung a cry of anguish from his lips. Shakily, he groped for the hidden obstruction, and his fingers clawed on the door of a car. He sobbed thankfully and wrenched at the handle, and the door flew open with a suddenness that surprised him. He was just in time. A circle of light broke the gloom as he flung himself forward, and Paul, carrying the constable's torch, cried jubilantly: 'Got you, you swine! Got you!'

But Paul had spoken too soon.

Instinctively, as he slid into the car, Ritchie had known that it was his own, and the knowledge was heartening. He groped feverishly for the cubby in the dashboard, and his fingers trembled as they closed over the coldness of a spanner. The car swayed as Paul leapt on the running-board, and Ritchie turned.

In a flash, Paul realised his danger. He had a brief glimpse of a raised arm; in that split second he knew only the fear and hate that was consuming the other . . . then the arm came swinging towards him.

There was only one thing to do. Dropping the torch, Paul grabbed at

Ritchie's arm, and with a mighty heave, he pulled Ritchie bodily out of the car. He didn't stand on ceremony. Ritchie, taken completely by surprise, was an open target, and before he had time to recover, Paul's fist came up with all the power behind it he could muster. There was no need for a second blow.

Ritchie gave just one gasp; then, staggering back against the car, he collapsed in a heap on the drive.

'That's in payment for the one you gave me!' breathed Paul with intense satisfaction; then he turned to meet the approaching constable.

★   ★   ★

It was the postman who awoke Paul the next morning. After a long session at the local police station the night before, he had been glad of some rest, and it seemed that no sooner had he lowered his head on the settee than the sound of a rattle at the letter-box disturbed him.

Realising that it was morning, he shook himself from his uneasy slumber and

198

looked about him. In the light of day, the sitting room looked even more chaotic than ever. Had all this really happened? thought Paul. Or was he still dreaming?

Finally, overwhelmed by curiosity, he went to the door and lifted the flap of the depository behind the letter-box. His groping fingers pulled out a long slender envelope and a postcard, and he looked at them perplexedly. Funny. The envelope wasn't addressed. Then how . . . ? Then it dawned on him that what the postman had brought that morning had been only a postcard, and that the envelope had been in the depository for some time.

Quickly, he tore open the envelope and withdrew the contents. If it was something for Peter, he supposed he'd better see what it was . . . Then he gasped. By the Lord Harry, it was the missing formula! And it had been here all the time! Of course. Wasn't the letter-box the obvious place to have looked for it?

He glanced ironically at the ransacked room. And Ritchie had gone to all this trouble — even to the length of murder — to gain possession of it. He'd have given anything to see Ritchie's face when he learned the truth. Oh well, at least the formula turning up would give him some excuse for seeing Jacqueline Marsden again . . .

The postcard was from Peter, telling him where to get his provisions, and who to apply to for domestic help. Paul absorbed all this absently. Then he caught sight of a postscript at the foot of the card, and he grinned. Grinned, then chuckled. Chuckled, then laughed. For the postscript said blithely:

'Hope you won't find it *too* quiet!'

MURDER BECOMES
A HABIT

1

It was a typically busy day at *Maison Gabriel*, the fashionable London ladies' hairdressing salon. At the small counter, the young receptionist Jean Carter was talking on the telephone. Her tone was polite and deferential:

'Miss Susann is free tomorrow morning at eleven-fifteen, Lady Panton . . . Oh yes, she's one of our best assistants . . . I quite understand that you'd rather have Mr. Gabriel, but you see, it *is* rather short notice, and . . . You'll come tomorrow morning . . . ? Very well, I'll book you an appointment with Miss Susann for eleven-fifteen. I'm quite sure you'll be satisfied . . . Thank you, Lady Panton . . . Goodbye.'

Jean sighed, wrinkled her nose, and permitted herself a tight little smile at having successfully dealt with another difficult caller. She replaced the receiver and began writing in the appointment book.

Behind her desk, Susann Ingram, the salon's chief assistant, was approaching one of the curtained cubicles. She was an attractive, sophisticated-looking girl in her late twenties, and wore a white nylon overall with the initials 'M.G.' stylishly affixed on her breast pocket. Smiling faintly, she swished back the curtain and entered the cubicle.

A woman was seated in the chair, her head partially concealed in the helmet-like hair dryer, which was switched on and humming softly. A magazine which she had been reading lay discarded on the floor.

Susann bent down and picked the magazine up, replaced it on a small recessed shelf by the chair.

'Now, Mrs. Radford, I think it's time we — ' She broke off abruptly, looking intently at the figure in the chair.

It was suspiciously still.

Tentatively, Susann touched the woman on the shoulder. 'Mrs. Radford, are you all right?'

There was no reply from Mrs. Radford. Suddenly, her outstretched hand flopped off the arm of the chair, and hung limply down the side.

* * *

Back at the reception area, the salon's owner, immaculate in his white jacket, was approaching the desk alongside one of his wealthy regular customers. He was a man in his middle forties, his bouffant hairstyle giving him a somewhat effeminate appearance. He smiled down on his customer, an over-dressed woman of uncertain years.

'You look exquisite, Mrs. Mannering, simply *exquisite*!' Gabriel enthused in an affected manner. 'Definitely one of my successful creations!'

'You — you *really* think it suits me?' Mrs. Mannering simpered doubtfully.

'My dear lady, it's you — absolutely *you*! So chic, and yet so unstudied! Just that touch of careless rapture that is essentially *your* ego! We — ' He broke off, frowning, at the clattering sound of hurried footsteps.

'Mr. Gabriel!' Susann cried excitedly.

'What is it, Miss Susann?'

'Could you come to Mrs. Radford? I — I'm afraid she's ill . . .'

Gabriel tensed, alarmed at Susann's agitated tone and the serious expression on her face. Then he turned to the open-mouthed Mrs. Mannering.

'Excuse me, Mrs. Mannering,' he said hastily. 'I hope you have a *wonderful* party.' He beckoned to his receptionist. 'Jean here will look after you, Mrs. Mannering . . .'

Gabriel moved off with Susann towards the cubicles at the back of the salon. 'What's the matter with Mrs. Radford?' he demanded, keeping his voice low.

Susann wrinkled her brow. 'I don't know. Her face is all swollen, and such a peculiar colour . . .'

'Oh dear! I do hope it's nothing serious . . . Perhaps the dryer was too hot?'

Susann shook her head. 'I turned it down to medium about fifteen minutes ago. She was all right then.'

They reached the cubicle, and Susann swished the curtain aside. Gabriel pushed past her and leant over the chair, looking closely at the unmoving figure beneath the dryer.

He straightened, thoroughly alarmed. 'Goodness, this is terrible! Quick, Susann, help me get this thing away.'

Susann switched off the humming dryer as Gabriel carefully raised the hood. Then, as Susann wheeled the dryer away to one side, Mrs. Radford began to slide out of the chair.

'Oh — she's going to fall!' Susann cried.

Moving quickly, Gabriel caught the woman's limp figure and settled it safely back in the chair again. He shot a glance at his assistant.

'Go and tell Jean to telephone for a doctor. Tell her to say it's urgent. And Susann — be quiet about it!'

Susann hesitated by the curtain. 'What's the matter with her?'

Gabriel straightened up. 'I'm afraid she's — dead!'

They stared at each other in consternation.

★ ★ ★

Detective Superintendent Merritt, C.I.D., was listening carefully to a police doctor in the now-crowded *Maison Gabriel*. They were standing by the reception counter. Behind them, to the rear of the salon, swirled the murmuring sounds of police activity and the subdued tones of shocked staff and clients.

'The woman died as the result of a quick-acting poison; introduced into the bloodstream,' the doctor told him, 'by means of a hypodermic needle.'

'That was the mark I saw on her neck?' Merritt asked.

The doctor nodded. 'Yes. It was made by the needle. At a guess, I should say curare. That would paralyse the respiratory system and prevent her being able to call out. I can't be certain of the poison, of course, until after the autopsy.'

Merritt sighed heavily. 'Charming case, I must say.' He frowned thoughtfully. 'I suppose death would have been pretty quick after the injection, wouldn't it, Doctor?'

'Practically instantaneous,' the doctor agreed. 'What's on your mind, Superintendent?'

'I was wondering whether it could be suicide . . . '

The doctor shook his head emphatically.

'Apart from the position of the neck-wound, what did she do with the hypodermic? It wasn't in the cubicle, was it?'

'No. That was the first thing we looked for.'

The doctor smiled grimly. 'So you can rule out suicide.'

'Which leaves — murder!'

'Exactly.' The doctor glanced about him. 'And I wish you joy of it. You've got the whole staff and an entire gaggle of women to choose from!'

'Thanks!' Merritt grunted.

'Don't mention it. Y'know, this is going to make quite a stir. Marian Radford was something of a V.I.P. American, rolling in money, intimate friend of all the best people . . . '

Merritt made a face. 'Don't I know it!'

The doctor reached for the bag he'd placed on the reception desk. 'Well, I'll leave you to get busy. I'll arrange with your pathologist for the post-mortem. How soon can we have the body?'

'Whenever you like. We've got all the photographs we want.'

'Good!' The doctor began to move away. 'You'll get the report as soon as we've done the job.'

'Thanks.' Merritt raised a hand as something occurred to him. 'Oh, Doctor, just one more thing . . . That poison you mentioned — I take it that it wouldn't be very easy to get hold of?'

'Not at all easy. Anything else?' As Merritt shook his head, the doctor turned towards the door again. 'So long, see you later.'

As he moved off, he nodded to Detective Sergeant Bates, who was approaching the counter. 'Hello, Bates. Got all the birds in your aviary under control?'

'Partially,' Bates answered, grimacing. 'Some of 'em are kicking up hell's delight at not being allowed to leave.'

After the doctor had left, Bates looked at his superior. 'Gabriel himself is almost in hysterics.'

'That's just too bad, Bates,' Merritt

smiled without humour, 'because I want to see him — right now. Has he a private office or anything?'

'Yes, sir.' Bates pointed to a door in the far corner of the salon. 'Over there. He's in there now.'

'Right. Arrange for the removal of the body, will you, then go and see what you can do to keep the customers quiet. Each of them will have to be searched before they can leave . . . '

Bates looked uncomfortable. 'That's going to put the cat among the pigeons, sir!'

Merritt shrugged. 'Can't help it. Better get hold of a couple of WPCs to do the job, or there *will* be a row!' he said dryly. 'They'll be looking for a hypodermic syringe — you know the sort of thing I mean.'

'Yes, sir.' Bates looked relieved.

'Cut along, then. I'm going to see our Mr. Gabriel.'

Reaching Gabriel's office door, Merritt tried the door handle, only to find it locked. He rapped sharply on the panel.

Gabriel's high-pitched voice sounded

behind the door. 'Who is it? What do you want?'

'Detective Superintendent Merritt, sir. I want a word with you.'

'Yes, yes, of course. One moment, Superintendent . . .'

Merritt heard a key turning in the lock, then Gabriel opened the door, peering round it.

'*Do* come in. I simply *had* to be alone for a moment,' Gabriel gushed. 'This has completely shattered my nerves — completely!'

Merritt stepped into the office and glanced around. There was a large desk with recessed compartments in its top, and a telephone. There was a small safe, and a couple of chairs. His gaze came back to the wretched Gabriel, and he forced sympathy into his voice.

'It must have been very trying for you, sir . . .'

'Trying?' Gabriel rolled his eyes. 'It's positively disastrous! I shall be ruined! Why, oh why, did that woman have to die in my salon?'

'I don't imagine she had any choice,

sir,' Merritt commented dryly.

'What will all my clients think? This has always been an exclusive establishment — a synonym for all that is best in style and taste.'

Merritt frowned impatiently. 'Quite, sir. Now, if you wouldn't mind answering a few questions . . . '

'I'll do my best, Superintendent, but I feel *drained*! Yes, that describes it perfectly — drained!' Gabriel returned to the seat behind his desk, and slumped into it as Merritt eased himself into another chair opposite it. He hitched himself around until he was directly facing the salon owner.

'I'll be as brief as I can, sir. When you found Mrs. Radford was ill, you sent for a doctor?'

'But of course! What else could I — '

'Quite so! It was at Doctor Mitchell's suggestion that the police were notified?'

Gabriel nodded, dabbing at his brow with a handkerchief. 'He was so sure she'd been poisoned. I can't believe it's really true . . . '

'I'm afraid it is, sir. She was poisoned all right, and the poison was administered by a hypodermic syringe . . . '

'Incredible — completely incredible!'

'Maybe, but it actually happened. Was the dead woman a regular customer here?'

'Mrs. Radford was one of my most valued clients. A charming lady — charming! Not in the first full flush of youthful maidenhood, but — '

'Exactly, sir,' Merritt cut short the effusions. 'I should say she was about forty-eight or fifty . . . ?'

'I make it a habit *never* to enquire into the age of my clients. Such a very delicate subject!'

'I understand she was recently married?'

'Oh, yes — about three months ago. Such a charming man — almost a perfect Grecian profile, and the most wonderful wave in his hair . . . '

Merritt frowned. 'He was much younger than she, wasn't he?'

'The heart can be young in spite of the passing years . . . '

At that moment, the door opened and Sergeant Bates appeared on the threshold.

'Excuse me, sir,' Bates began.

'What is it, Bates?' Merritt was thankful for the interruption.

'There's a woman in the salon who was a friend of Mrs. Radford's, sir.'

Gabriel jerked upright in consternation. 'Sara Graham! Oh dear, I forgot *she* was here. Now this will be all over London.'

Merritt looked at him sharply. 'Why?'

'She's a journalist, sir,' Bates told him, and added: 'She's a society gossip writer.'

'Such a vitriolic pen, too!' Gabriel shuddered.

'All right, Bates — wheel her in!'

'Yes, sir.' Bates exited the room, closing the door behind him.

Merritt turned to Gabriel. 'Was this woman, Miss Graham, very friendly with Mrs. Radford?'

'As friendly as two women can be, Superintendent. There's always a hint of claws, you know!'

The door opened and Sergeant Bates reappeared.

'This is Miss Graham, sir.'

Bates stepped aside to allow Sara Graham to enter the room, then withdrew and closed the door behind him.

Merritt regarded the new arrival with interest. She was a smartly dressed young woman of about thirty, attractive but rather hard-faced. He got up quickly to fetch another chair from a corner of the room, which he placed near to his own. Gabriel remained where he was behind his desk, looking somewhat apprehensive.

Sara advanced towards them and slipped into her seat. 'Thank you, Superintendent . . . It's perfectly ghastly about Marian. What actually happened?'

Instead of answering her directly, Merritt asked: 'You knew Mrs. Radford very well, I understand?'

'Yes. I've known her for several years.'

'Had she any enemies?'

Sara raised her eyebrows. 'I don't know what you mean by 'enemies'. A woman in Marian's position always arouses a certain amount of envy and malice . . . '

'I was thinking of something more than that,' Merritt told her. 'Do you know of anybody who had threatened to kill her — who would wish to kill her?'

Sara blinked. 'Are you telling me

216

Marian was *murdered*?'

'Yes, I'm afraid she was.'

Gabriel wrung his hands. 'Isn't it dreadful? In *my* salon . . . '

Sara was aghast. 'I don't understand. How could anyone have . . . ?'

'We shall come to that later, Miss Graham,' Merritt said. 'Tell me, what kind of woman was Mrs. Radford?'

'Kind of woman?'

'Would you say she was pleasant, likeable . . . ?'

'She was charming — perfectly charming!' Gabriel said.

'Not always,' Sara was quick to correct him.

'What do you mean by that, Miss Graham?' Merritt asked sharply.

'Well, she was generous and warm-hearted, but she *could* be rather hard and obstinate. It depended on whether she liked you or not . . . '

'But surely we are all like that?' Gabriel protested. 'She was sweet — perfectly sweet!'

'You didn't know her as well as I did!'

Merritt changed the subject. 'Do you

know her husband, Miss Graham?'

'Adrian? Of course. He was her fourth husband, you know. Her first two husbands died — one in the war. They were Americans. Her third husband, she divorced. He's an Englishman — Monty Beresford. Full of charm, but always getting into scrapes over money. He drinks heavily, too. Marian was constantly getting him out of trouble, even after the divorce.'

'I see. He lives in London?'

'Yes. I can give you his address, if you want it.'

'Give it to Sergeant Bates, Miss Graham. Her last marriage, I believe, was quite recent?'

'Oh, yes.' Sara smiled sardonically. 'Quite a whirlwind affair! She met Adrian Radford at a cocktail party, and they were married a week later. Quite ridiculous! Adrian was only thirty, and Marian knew absolutely nothing about him.' She shrugged and spread her hands. 'But she was infatuated, and wouldn't listen to reason.'

'Adrian Radford is so good-looking!' Gabriel interjected.

'If you like that type of good looks!'

Sara commented dryly.

'You don't, Miss Graham?' Merritt asked.

'No, I don't. I've nothing against Adrian . . . '

'But you don't like him?'

'Not very much. Have you told him — about Marian?'

'Not yet,' Merritt admitted.

'He'll be a very, very wealthy man now . . . ' Sara suddenly looked at her watch. 'Do you think I could go, Superintendent? I'm already late for a rather important appointment . . . '

'I'm afraid I shall have to ask you to wait a little longer,' Merritt told her.

Sara frowned. 'It's very inconvenient . . . '

'A murder investigation is always inconvenient to quite a lot of people, Miss Graham,' Merritt told her, glancing round as he heard the door open to admit Sergeant Bates.

'We're getting on with the search, sir, but we haven't found anything yet,' Bates admitted.

'Keep at it. You might see if you can finish with Miss Graham quickly — she's in rather a hurry.'

'All right, sir.' Bates glanced at Sara. 'If you'll come with me, Miss Graham . . . '

Sara stood up with alacrity. 'Thank you, Superintendent.'

'We try to make it as easy as possible, Miss Graham.' He looked at Bates. 'I want to see the girl who made the discovery of Mrs. Radford's body, Bates. Send her in, will you?'

'Right, sir.'

As they prepared to leave, Merritt added: 'Give Sergeant Bates that address you mentioned, Miss Graham, will you?'

'Of course. Goodbye, Superintendent. Goodbye, Gabriel.'

Gabriel shook his head sadly. 'I am desolate, Miss Graham. My soul is mourning for the death of my business.'

Sara turned at the doorway and gave him a slightly contemptuous glance. 'Don't be silly! You'll survive!'

As the door closed behind her, Gabriel sighed heavily. 'She doesn't understand . . . Nobody understands how an artist can suffer! I must go and pacify my clients. This is the most wretched day of my life!'

Merritt tightened his lips, and decided that he had got everything useful from Gabriel for the moment. 'You can go too, if you like. But I may want to talk to you later.'

There was a tap on the door and Susann Ingram entered the room.

Merritt smiled, and nodded towards the seat Sara had vacated.

'You want to see me?' Susann asked, as she seated herself.

'Yes. Your name is Ingram — Susann Ingram — isn't it?'

The girl hesitated, watching Gabriel pass her on his way out. She waited until he had closed the door behind him before answering.

'Actually, it's Susan Ingram, but Mr. Gabriel thought that 'Susann' sounded better.'

'Well, we'll stick to Susann, shall we?' Merritt decided. 'Now, Miss Susann, you were the first person to find that there was something wrong with Mrs. Radford, weren't you?'

'Yes.'

'Will you tell me exactly what happened?'

'Well, Mrs. Radford had an appointment for a shampoo and set at three-thirty . . . '

'One moment,' Merritt interrupted. 'Did *you* always attend to Mrs. Radford when she came here?'

'Yes, partly.'

Merritt frowned. 'What do you mean — partly?'

'If it was styling or anything elaborate,' Susann explained, 'then I only assisted Mr. Gabriel.'

'I see . . . Go on, please. What happened this afternoon?'

'Mrs. Radford was a little late for her appointment. It was twenty minutes to four before she arrived. I gave her a shampoo and set, and put her under the dryer while I went to comb out another client . . . '

'Leaving Mrs. Radford alone in the cubicle?' Merritt asked sharply.

'Yes.'

'With the curtains drawn?'

'Yes. The dryer was turned on full, and after about fifteen minutes I came back and put it down to medium.'

'Was Mrs. Radford all right then?'

'Yes. She was reading one of our magazines. I went back to my other client, and about a quarter of an hour later I returned to Mrs. Radford to comb her out. The magazine was on the floor, and she — she looked dreadful . . . '

'Did you know she was dead?'

'Mr. Gabriel said she was. I was too horrified to look . . . '

Merritt nodded sympathetically. 'It must have been a nasty shock for you. The cubicle she was in isn't visible from the receptionist's desk, is it? So anyone could have slipped in while you were away?'

'Yes, I suppose they could,' the girl admitted. 'I was at the other end of the salon.'

'So you wouldn't be able to see or hear anything that took place in Mrs. Radford's cubicle?' Merritt pressed.

'No.'

'Did you move anything in the cubicle after you found Mrs. Radford dead?'

'Mr. Gabriel asked me to move the dryer back a little, that's all.'

'You didn't take anything away?'

Merritt asked sharply.

'Certainly not.'

'Did you see Mr. Gabriel remove anything?'

'No.'

Merritt digested this information. Then: 'During the time you were waiting for the doctor, was there anyone with Mrs. Radford?'

'I don't know. Mr. Gabriel told me to go back and finish my other client. He told me not to say that there was anything wrong.'

'Thank you, Miss Susann. I think that's all for the present.'

'Thank you.'

Merritt rose to his feet as the girl got up, and accompanied her to the door. From the open doorway, he called out: 'Bates!'

'Coming, sir!' Bates was on the far side of the salon, in the reception area. He hastened to join his superior as Merritt came out of the office and closed the door.

'Nearly finished with them all out there, Bates?'

'Nearly, sir. No luck. There's no sign of a hypodermic on any of 'em.'

'H'm. Better let the customers go. Have you searched the staff?'

'I was going to do that next, sir.'

'The whole place will have to be combed. We've got to find that hypodermic.'

'I've arranged for that to be done. Oh, there's one thing, sir. The receptionist was away from her desk for nearly ten minutes, in the staff-room making tea.'

'What time was this?'

'Just before that girl, Susann, gave the alarm, sir.'

Merritt frowned. 'So anybody could have slipped in or out without being seen, eh?'

'Yes, sir.'

'Just to make it more difficult.' Merritt grunted. 'Oh well, get everything organised here, then we'll go and interview the husband.'

'He ought to be the chief suspect,' Bates commented.

'According to the book — yes. But I don't think it's going to be as easy as that!'

2

Adrian Radford was splashing whisky from a decanter into his glass. He appeared disturbed, for he gulped his drink quickly. He stood for a moment to regain his composure, before turning to face the two visitors in his luxurious London flat.

Having delivered their news of his wife's death, Superintendent Merritt and Sergeant Bates waited respectfully for him to speak.

'I'm sorry, Superintendent, but I needed that! This has given me a terrible shock!' Radford's handsome face was haggard as he ran a hand through his thick, wavy hair.

'I can understand that, Mr. Radford,' Merritt said.

Radford moved agitatedly about the room. 'It — it seems so impossible — so utterly impossible! Marian and I were ... going to a party this evening. I couldn't . . . understand why she was so long . . . '

'I'm sorry to have to worry you in the circumstances, sir, but I'm sure you'll realise the police have to . . . ' Merritt paused.

'Of course. Nothing must be neglected that will bring the person who did this damnable thing to justice . . . Oh, forgive me! Perhaps you and your — er — confrère would like a drink?'

'No, thank you, sir. Has your wife been as usual lately?' As Merritt spoke, Bates surreptitiously produced a small note-book.

Radford halted his pacing.

'Had you noticed any signs that she was worried or upset?' Merritt prompted.

'No. She — she was just the same as usual. I can't imagine anyone wanting to — to harm her. She was such a — such a grand person . . . '

'Somebody thought differently, sir,' Merritt said grimly.

'If I could get my hands on the bastard . . . '

'Quite so, sir. I sympathise with your

227

feelings, but it isn't going to get us anywhere,' Merritt said levelly.

'I'm sorry,' Radford mumbled an apology. 'I'm all to pieces . . . '

Merritt waited a few moments, then continued his questioning in the same level tone.

'Can you suggest any motive for your wife's death, sir? Who benefits?'

'Well, there's me, of course, Marian made no secret of the fact that she's left me the bulk of her fortune . . . '

'Apart from you, sir?'

'There was Beresford — he's her divorced husband, you know — '

Merritt nodded.

'She left him something — a few thousand, I believe. A thoroughly dissolute scoundrel — always sponging off her . . . '

'Anyone else?' Merritt prompted.

Radford wrinkled his brow. 'I think Sara Graham was left a legacy. I don't know . . . The solicitors will be able to give you all the information you want about that.'

Bates looked up from his notebook.

'Will you give me the name and address, sir?'

'Witherfield, Handshot and Witherfield, Bedford Row . . . '

'Thank you, sir.' Bates scribbled down the address in his notebook.

Radford moistened his lips. 'Do you mind if I have another drink?' He went over to the table and refilled his glass from the decanter. Merritt watched him narrowly.

'Sir, I hope you won't take this amiss, but we've got to check on everything, and . . . '

Radford turned and regarded him. 'You want to know what I've been doing all afternoon, Superintendent?'

'From, say, three-forty-five until five-thirty, sir.'

Radford smiled faintly. 'That's easy.' He took a long drink. 'I was here. I haven't been out since lunchtime.'

'Alone, sir?'

'Luckily for me, no! I had a friend with me . . . '

Bates poised his pencil. 'Who was that, sir?'

'Frank Layton. He owns a wine business in Bond Street — Senior and Layton. He'll substantiate my — er — alibi.'

As Bates entered the address in his notebook, there came the distant sound of door chimes.

Merritt raised an eyebrow. 'Alibi is rather a strong way of putting it, sir, at present.'

Radford put down his glass and smiled sardonically. 'The husband is always suspected in the case of a wife as rich as Marian. Isn't that true?'

Merritt shrugged. 'In most cases, yes, sir. But . . .'

He broke off as the door opened and Radford's manservant appeared.

'Will you see Miss Graham, sir?'

Radford smiled broadly. 'Sara . . . Show her in, Chub!'

At that moment Sara Graham swept past Chub. The manservant withdrew, closing the door behind him.

Sara strode half-way across the room and halted to survey the assembly. She gave a slight smile.

'I came to break the news to you, Adrian, but I see I've been forestalled.'

'We're just going, Miss Graham,' Merritt said. 'Thanks for your help, Mr Radford. We may want to see you again.'

'Any time . . . ' Radford spoke abstractedly, his eyes on Sara. 'If there's anything at all I can do, just let me know . . . '

'You can depend on that, sir.' Merritt followed Bates, who opened the door to the vestibule. He paused and turned in the doorway as Radford moved forward.

'Don't trouble to see us out,' Merritt told him. 'Goodnight, Miss Graham. Goodnight, sir.'

'Goodnight.' Radford and Sara Graham spoke together.

Merritt and Bates left the flat, and moved towards the lift gates at the end of the corridor.

Bates gave his superior a sideways glance. 'Well, sir, what's your opinion of Radford?'

'What's yours?' Merritt countered.

Bates blew out his cheeks. 'Quite an eyeful, but I wasn't impressed.'

'Didn't quit ring true, eh?' Merritt

wrinkled his brow. 'I wonder if *this* was Miss Graham's important appointment?'

Bates nodded. 'She wouldn't have had much time for any other, sir.'

They arrived at the lift gates, and Merritt pressed the button to summon the lift.

'And she said she didn't like Radford. H'm! It might be worth looking a bit closer at Miss Graham, Bates . . . '

★　★　★

Back in Radford's lounge, he was looking at Sara appraisingly as she seated herself on the settee, and began to slowly withdraw her gloves. He moved towards her.

'Sara . . . my dear . . . '

She looked up at him coolly. 'I'd like a drink — a large brandy.'

'Of course . . . ' Radford crossed to the table and poured out a brandy. Quickly, he brought it over to her at the settee. She took it from him without a word. Radford looked down at her as she sipped from her glass, then seated himself beside her.

'Sara . . . It was sweet of you to come . . . '

She edged away from him and regarded him coldly across the rim of her glass.

'Yes . . . wasn't it?'

★ ★ ★

The next day, the sound of Big Ben chiming the half-hour could be faintly heard in Merritt's office at Scotland Yard, through the window overlooking the Embankment. Detective Sergeant Bates busied himself arranging papers on the superintendent's desk. He was whistling a popular tune as the door opened and his superior entered.

'You sound cheerful this morning, Bates.'

Bates shrugged. 'I've no particular reason for being cheerful, sir.'

Merritt turned back to his desk as he finished hanging up his hat and coat. 'Just keeping your spirits up, eh? Pity! I was hoping you'd have some good news for me . . . What's all this stuff you're putting on my desk?'

'Reports, mostly.' Bates selected one. 'Here's the result of the autopsy on the dead woman, sir.'

Merritt seated himself at his desk and accepted the paper that was offered to him.

Bates settled in a chair and waited while the superintendent studied the report.

'H'm . . . so the poison was cobra venom, eh?' Merritt looked up at Bates. 'That's a new one — new to me, anyhow.'

'And not very easy to get hold of, sir.'

'That may help us. We'll check up on the supplies in the country. Smithson can do that . . . Any sign of the hypodermic?'

Bates sighed. 'No, sir. The hairdressing salon has been practically under a microscope. Our men worked until the early hours, but they didn't find anything.'

'Did the search include the safe in the office?'

'Yes, sir. They got the key from Gabriel. He was a bit difficult about it . . . '

Merritt smiled. 'I can imagine. I wonder what happened to the syringe? Surely none of the staff or the customers could have smuggled it out . . . '

'That's true, sir. They were each searched separately before they left.'

Merritt smacked his palm on the desk in frustration. 'And nobody — repeat, *nobody* — left that salon after Mrs. Radford was killed. We've checked that. So what the devil happened to that hypodermic?'

Bates shook his head. 'You can ask that again, sir!'

'And I shall keep on asking until we know, Bates. What about Adonis's alibi?'

'Adonis, sir?'

'The beautiful Mr. Radford!'

Bates spread his hands. 'Clean bill! Layton was with him, as he said.'

Merrill sighed. 'I didn't expect anything else. According to all the rules, Radford ought to be the murderer, but I don't think he is.'

'So far as motive goes . . . '

'I've got a whole selection of motives for you, Bates. I've seen the dead woman's solicitors this morning. She was worth over four and a half million.'

Bates whistled. 'That's money, sir.'

'Her father was a millionaire; her first husband was another,' Merritt elaborated. 'She inherited the lot . . . '

'And Radford gets it?

'The bulk of it. Sara Graham gets ten thousand; the divorced husband, Beresford, gets five thousand. There are quite a number of smaller bequests to friends and old servants in America which don't concern us, and various sums to charities . . . '

'Radford was right about Beresford and Graham . . . '

'Yes, and the legacies put them among our gallery of suspects — particularly Sara Graham, who was in the hairdressing salon at the time.'

Merritt examined more of the reports on his desk. At length, he said, 'But that isn't all, my lad. Marian Radford was contemplating issuing a writ on Gabriel for the repayment of a loan of seven thousand pounds. What do you think of that, eh?'

'Gabriel!' Bates exclaimed. 'That makes another suspect who was on the spot, sir.'

'Exactly.'

Bates frowned. 'Hold on a minute, though. Her death wouldn't save him from having to repay the money to the estate . . . '

'In this case, it would. There's a clause in the will absolving all persons who owed her money from repayment in the event of her death.'

'So it was a bit of luck for Gabriel that she died, sir.'

'Seven thousand bits of luck.'

'And he had the opportunity.'

'But did he have any cobra venom, or was he in a position to get hold of any?' Merritt furrowed his brow as he grappled with the conflicting issues this case was throwing up. 'We're coming up against a snag there, Bates. And what happened to the hypodermic . . . ? By the way, there's another name for that poison — where's that report?' He scanned hastily down a page. 'Oh, here it is . . . colubrine — that's the stuff. And you can't just walk into the nearest chemist and buy it!'

'It wouldn't be used for any form of beauty preparation or hair dye, I suppose, sir?' Bates hazarded.

'I should hardly think so. But we'll get the experts on to it . . . You've got Beresford's address, haven't you?'

'Yes, sir.'

Merritt rose to his feet. 'Right. Then get your coat. We'll go and have a word with him.'

★ ★ ★

The C.I.D. squad car pulled up outside a dingy block of downmarket flats in a second-class area of London. Merritt and Bates alighted from the car, and headed for the entrance to the building.

On finding their way to Beresford's flat, Bates knocked on the door.

There was no response. He exchanged a glance with Merritt and repeated the operation — to no effect.

'Can't be at home, sir.'

'Doesn't look like it, does it? Give it another tattoo, then we'll call it a day.'

Bates knocked thunderously on the door

Merritt smiled. 'If that doesn't get an answer, we'll — '

He broke off at the sudden sound of

uneven footsteps from inside the flat. At length, the door was opened by Montague Beresford. The C.I.D. men stared at him interestedly.

Beresford was a dark, slight man in his middle thirties, wearing reasonably well-cut clothes that had once been well-cared-for. But that was obviously quite some time ago; now he was dressed carelessly, and had the air of a man who was rapidly going to seed. He peered at them irritably. When he spoke, his voice was slurred with drink.

'What the hell are you kicking up such a damn row for?'

'Mr. Beresford?' Merritt suppressed his distaste as he put the question.

'Yes. What do you want?'

'We're police officers . . . ' Merritt began, but Beresford cut him short.

'If you've come from Jacobson, you can go back and tell him he'll get his money . . . '

'We're investigating the murder of Mrs. Radford, sir.'

'Marian . . . ' Beresford whispered the name as if it meant something to him, and just for a moment he showed a flicker of emotion he was unable to suppress. Then it passed.

Merritt spoke firmly. 'Can we come in, sir?'

Beresford shrugged and held the door open wider. 'Come in if you want to,' he muttered.

The two C.I.D. men entered the flat via a tiny hall with no great enthusiasm. They passed into a small, untidy-looking living room. The chairs were littered with newspapers and the remains of a meal were still on the table. Alongside it was a half-empty packet of cigarettes, and an ashtray full of cigarette ends.

Behind them, Beresford blurted out: 'It's not me you want to see, you know. It's Radford . . . '

'We've already seen Mr. Radford, sir,' Bates informed him.

'You've got him, have you?' Beresford said excitedly. 'The swine! I hope you hang him!' He ushered them further into the room. 'Come in here. We'll have a drink on it!'

'Not for us, sir,' Merritt said briefly.

'Well, *I* want one.'

Beresford pushed the door shut and lurched over to the table. Unsteadily, he uncorked a bottle and poured himself a drink. Merritt and Bates exchanged glances.

'It'd be better if you wait until we'd finished, sir . . . ' Merritt began.

'Can't wait, old boy. Sorry you won't join me.' Beresford raised his glass in a salute. 'Here's eternal damnation to that sleek, wavy-haired snake . . . '

He drank greedily.

'You think it was Mr. Radford who killed his wife, sir?' Bates asked.

'Who else would've done it, eh?' Beresford demanded. 'He gets all the money, doesn't he? That's what he married her for — the money. I told her she was a fool, but she wouldn't listen. In — *infatuated* — that's what she was — with that blasted Greek profile . . . '

'It couldn't have been Mr. Radford,' Merritt said levelly.

'Couldn't've been?' Beresford glared at him blearily. 'What do you mean — couldn't've been? It *was*, I tell you. No one else would've wanted to harm Marian. I thought you'd got him . . . '

'Mr. Radford has an alibi,' Bates explained. 'He wasn't near the hairdressing salon . . . '

'Alibi — alibi? To hell with his alibi! Cunning as a monkey . . . Pull the wool over the eyes of an angel. He did. Marian was an angel — damned good sort. Too good for me . . . We didn't hit it off, but it wasn't her fault . . . Always in trouble. Couldn't keep off this stuff . . . ' Beresford's outburst subsided as he turned to the table and helped himself to another drink.

'She was going to help me out again,' he resumed. 'S'posed to meet her at that hairdressing place . . . '

'Yesterday afternoon?' Merritt asked sharply.

'That's right. Give me the money to pay off that swine Jacobson. That's the sort of woman she was. Heart as big as a — a castle . . . '

He drank noisily.

Merritt was watching him keenly. 'You were going to meet Mrs. Radford yesterday afternoon?'

'I told you so, didn't I?'

'At *Maison Gabriel*?'

'That's where she was, wasn't it?'

'What time were *you* there sir?'

Beresford shrugged. 'I dunno — I got held up . . . ' He peered ruminatively into his glass. 'Ran into Sara — Sara Graham — just as I got there. She told me what had happened . . . Shook me up . . . '

Merritt frowned. 'You didn't enter the salon?'

'I've told you, I met Sara,' Beresford slurred. 'She told me Marian was dead. What was the point of going into the place?'

'Did you know that Mrs. Radford had left you five thousand pounds in her will?' Merritt asked sharply.

'Of course I did. Marian told me . . . Look here, what's the good of questioning *me*? You go after Radford. He's the man you want.'

'We have to check up on everybody, sir,' Merritt said patiently.

'You con — *concentrate* on Radford. Concentrate like hell. I may be a bit woozy, but I know what I'm talking about.' He poured himself another drink.

'We shan't overlook anything,' Merritt said briefly.

'That's right . . . Poor old Marian! Unlucky in her choice of men, eh? Don't s'pose it matters to her now . . . Sure you won' have a drink?' Beresford waved the bottle unsteadily.

'No, thank you, sir. We've still got a lot of work to do, so — ' He broke off as there sounded a knocking at the door.

'Now who the devil's that?' Beresford slurred irritably. 'Ex — excuse me.' He put down his glass and lurched out of the room into the hall.

Bates watched his erratic progress and shook his head. 'He's liable to pass out at any minute, sir.'

'Yes. I don't think we can do much good here,' Merritt said, low-voiced.

They listened to Beresford fumbling with the door before finally getting it open.

'Hello! C-come in,' Beresford's voice sounded from the hall. 'Join the party!

'The party?' The C.I.D. men recognised the surprised voice of Sara Graham.

'Got — two p'licemen here. Come on in . . .'

As Sara entered the room she saw Beresford's visitors. 'Oh! You're quite ubiquitous, aren't you, Superintendent?'

'That seems to apply equally to you, Miss Graham,' Merritt responded dryly.

'I hope I'm not interrupting anything?' the girl said.

''Course you're not. Have a drink. There's whisky, gin . . .'

'No thanks, Monty.'

'You didn't tell us you met Mr. Beresford outside *Maison Gabriel* yesterday afternoon, Miss Graham,' Merritt said.

Sara glanced at Beresford. 'Did he tell you that?'

'Yes. Why didn't you mention it?'

'I didn't want to say anything in front of Adrian . . .'

Beresford gave an angry grimace. 'Adrian — Adrian? Have you seen that smarmy swine? He did it, you know. He killed Marian . . .'

'Don't be silly, Monty!' Sara snapped.

'You don't believe me, do you? None of

you believe me.' Beresford shrugged. 'Never mind — let's have another drink . . . '

He moved towards a second bottle.

'You've had enough already, Monty,' Sara admonished.

'Nonsense! I'm all right . . . '

Sara tightened her lips. 'I came to talk to you — sensibly. But I'm clearly wasting my time.'

'Talk — sensibly?' Beresford blinked. 'What about?'

'Never mind.' Sara turned to Merritt. 'Is there anything new, Superintendent? Or mustn't one ask?'

Instead of answering, Merritt asked a question of his own. 'Did you know that Mrs. Radford had left you ten thousand pounds, Miss Graham?'

'I did. Are you suggesting that *I* killed her?'

'I'm not suggesting anything — at the moment. I'm just collecting information.'

'I see.' Sara smiled grimly. 'Well, I'll give you this to add to your collection. Gabriel had a pretty good motive — and he also had the opportunity.'

'You mean the loan of seven thousand pounds?'

Sara looked at Merritt in surprise. 'You know about that?'

'Yes, Miss Graham, we know about that.'

'Do you also know that he takes drugs?'

'Drugs?' Merritt exchanged a startled glance with Bates.

'Yes — injections. Administered with a hypodermic, Superintendent!'

3

At the *Maison Gabriel*, receptionist Jean Carter seemed to be busier than ever. Susann Ingram, standing by the reception desk, was listening to her with an expression of amused sympathy.

'Yes, madam,' Jean was saying into the phone, 'I'm sure you would ... No, madam, it's quite impossible ... Yes, fully booked, I'm afraid ... No, madam, not the slightest — I'm sorry ... Good-bye ... '

She replaced the receiver impatiently and looked up at Susann.

'The phone's scarcely stopped ringing all morning. I should think nearly every woman in London wants to book an appointment!'

Susann shrugged. 'It's just morbid curiosity, that's all. I don't know how many times I've had to explain to customers exactly how I found poor Mrs. Radford.'

'That's why they want to come, Susann. They all ask for 'the girl who made the discovery'. Disgusting, I call it!'

Susann sighed heavily. 'I must say, I'm getting a bit tired of it myself. Going over and over it all again . . . '

The telephone rang for the umpteenth time that day. Jean glared at the instrument crossly.

'There! What did I tell you? It never stops!'

Susann turned to move away. 'Well, I must get back to my client. See you later . . . '

Jean nodded to her colleague as she lifted the receiver.

'*Maison Gabriel* . . . I'm very sorry, but we're absolutely booked up for the next fortnight . . . No, it's quite impossible, madam. I'm sorry.'

As she replaced the receiver, the entrance door opened; Bates walked in and approached her desk.

'Can I have a word with Mr. Gabriel? Detective Sergeant Bates . . . '

Jean looked at him doubtfully. 'I remember you . . . He's awfully busy . . . '

'It's rather important.' Bates' tone brooked no argument.

Jean rose from her seat. 'I'll go and tell him . . . '

As she turned, she caught sight of her employer emerging from his office.

'Oh, there he is. *Mr. Gabriel!*'

Gabriel hurried forward, looking distinctly harassed.

'What is it, Sergeant? I'm terribly busy . . . '

'There are one or two questions we should like you to answer, Mr. Gabriel,' Bates said stolidly.

'But I'm so tired of questions!' Gabriel waved a hand irritably. 'There are nothing but questions! Reporters asking questions, policemen asking questions. Questions, questions, ques- — '

'I won't keep you any longer than I can help, sir.'

'Must you bother me now? How can I concentrate on my creative work if I am constantly being inter- —'

'I'm afraid the matter is urgent, sir.

'Oh, very well. But be quick! I have two important clients . . . '

'Can we use your office, sir?' Bates nodded towards the back of the salon.

'I suppose so!' Gabriel sighed theatrically. 'It's really very trying! Jean, ask Miss Yvonne to start combing out Mrs. Noble, will you?'

He turned back towards his office, Bates following. 'Oh dear, I'm worn out — completely worn out!'

The telephone rang again, and Jean Carter spoke wearily: '*Maison Gabriel* . . . I'm very sorry, madam, but I'm afraid we can't book any more appointments . . . '

Gabriel closed his office door behind Bates. 'You heard? It's like that all the time. How can I cope with it?'

'That's up to you, sir,' Bates said shortly. 'I should like some information concerning a loan of seven thousand pounds made to you by Mrs. Radford.'

Gabriel stopped in his tracks and looked at Bates in surprise.

'How did you know about that?'

'We never divulge the source of our information, sir,' Bates said flatly.

Gabriel was indignant. 'It's intolerable! The matter was private! I refuse to discuss it — absolutely!'

Bates shrugged. 'Of course, you can refuse if you wish, sir. But it might be better to discuss it with me than in public.'

'In public? What do you mean?'

'If it has nothing to do with Mrs. Radford's death, sir, there's no reason why it shouldn't remain a private matter.'

Gabriel had reached his desk, and slumped into his chair. 'But how could it have anything to do with her death?'

Bates seated himself near the desk. 'I understand that Mrs. Radford was dissatisfied with the repayment of the loan, sir. She was contemplating proceedings against you.'

Gabriel stood up, thoroughly alarmed. 'I know what you are insinuating . . . You think I killed her . . . I killed her to avoid having to repay the loan? That's what the police believe . . . ?'

'Why should her death stop that, sir?' Bates said quietly.

'There was a clause in her will — ' Gabriel stopped abruptly.

'So you knew about that, sir?'

Gabriel looked uncomfortable. 'She

told me — I forget when . . . It's really monstrous to suggest that I killed her. I wouldn't kill anyone or anything. I abhor violence of any sort . . . '

'Quite so, sir,' Bates said levelly. He paused, then said sharply: 'Do you have, or have you had, in your possession a hypodermic syringe?'

Gabriel gave a distinct start. 'I definitely refuse to answer any further questions — quite definitely!'

Bates shrugged. 'You are at liberty to do that if you wish, sir.'

'And I shall consult my solicitor!' Gabriel snapped. 'You have no right to come here and accuse me of . . . '

'I haven't accused you anything, sir,' Bates said, getting to his feet.

'Not in so many words, perhaps, but your attitude . . . Oh dear, I feel *so* upset. My nerves are screaming — positively screaming! I shall be a complete wreck for the rest of the day!'

Bates turned to the door. 'Very well, sir. I won't worry you any more — *for the present.*'

The sergeant left the room. Gabriel had

not missed the emphasis in his final words. The interview had shaken his nerves.

He got up and locked his office door from the inside. Then he went back to his desk and moved the framed blotting-pad, opening a shallow compartment in the desk top which looked like part of the inlay.

From it, he took out a small bottle and a hypodermic syringe.

★   ★   ★

Detective Superintendent Merritt was working at his desk in his Scotland Yard office when one of his C.I.D. colleagues entered.

He was of small build, and his features nondescript, but there was a keen intelligence in his grey eyes that reflected the fact that he was an expert toxicologist, and quite one of the cleverest men at the Yard.

'You wanted to see me?'

Merritt looked up, smiling. 'Oh, come in, Smithson. I've got something right up your street. Pull that chair up and sit down.'

Smithson seated himself at the front of the desk. 'It's about this Radford murder, I take it?'

'That's right. I want to talk to you about this poison.'

'Cobra venom, eh?'

Merritt nodded. 'How could anyone get hold of the stuff?'

'Well, it'd be difficult. You might find some in a high-class research laboratory. Or maybe a hospital. It's been tried as a treatment for epilepsy, I believe, with a fair amount of success.'

'Could you find out where there are any supplies?' Merritt asked?

'Well, yes, I suppose I could.'

'If we know where this cobra venom — colubrine, or whatever it is — is available,' Merritt explained, 'we can check up on who among the people connected with this business would have been in a position to get hold of it.'

Smithson nodded thoughtfully. 'Wherever they kept even a small stock of the venom, it'd be strictly checked. If any was missing, it would be known almost at once.'

'Even if something else was substituted?'

'That might work,' Smithson conceded, 'but only if the venom wasn't used frequently.'

'Well, get busy and see what you can unearth. You're our tame toxicologist, so it's up to you.'

Smithson got to his feet. 'I'll do my best. Queer choice of poison to use — unless the murderer used it because he already *had* it.'

Merritt frowned. 'This is the first time I've come up against cobra venom.'

'It's not unique, you know. There was a case in which it was used about five years ago.'

'Is that so?' Merritt was interested. 'Murder?'

'I think so. Afraid I can't remember the details, offhand. Somewhere up North, I believe, and — ' Smithson broke off as the door opened and Sergeant Bates entered.

Smithson smiled. 'Hello, Bates! Doing

all the work while your boss relaxes in the office on his backside, eh?'

Bates grinned. 'Well, I wouldn't say that, sir.'

'You'd better not, my lad!' Merritt spoke with mock severity.

Smithson turned as he reached the door. 'I'll push off and get those inquiries you want under way. Let you know as soon as I have anything useful.'

'Thanks.' Merritt waited until the door closed, and then turned to Bates. 'Well, what did you get out of Gabriel?'

'Not much, sir,' Bates said as he took the vacant chair. 'He admitted that he knew all about that clause in the will . . . '

'That puts him in our top ten for suspects, anyway.'

'That's *all* I could get. He refused to answer any further questions about his use of a syringe. Said he was consulting his solicitor.'

'And we can't do a thing about it! He's within his rights!' Merritt smote his desk in disgust. 'Judges' rules! We're expected to get results, and they tie us up in red tape! Well, let's see what we've got so far.

Gabriel, the Graham woman, and Beresford are our chief suspects.'

'Beresford, sir?'

Merritt nodded. 'He had a pretty big motive, too . . . ' He smiled faintly. 'Don't look so surprised — you're not the only one who's been working today! Remember him mentioning somebody called Jacobson? Jacobson, it turns out, runs a shady little club off Shaftesbury Avenue. Beresford cashed a cheque with him for two hundred pounds a month ago. It was a post-dated cheque. I've got all the dope here.' He tapped a folder on his desk. 'The date had expired, and Jacobson wouldn't be stalled any longer. He insisted that he was going to pay it into the bank.'

'And it'd bounce, eh?'

'Worse than that, Bates. The signature on the cheque was supposed to be Mrs. Radford's!'

Bates gave a whistle. 'Forgery!'

'Exactly.'

'That's pretty serious . . . Hold on, sir. Beresford said that Mrs. Radford was going to give him the money . . . '

Merritt nodded. 'That's what he *said*. We've no evidence to back it up.'

'But he never entered the salon, sir,' Bates pointed out. 'He didn't get there until after Mrs. Radford was dead.'

'That could have been the *second* time, Bates. That receptionist — what's her name?'

'Jean Carter, sir.'

'She was away in the staff-room making tea. He could have slipped in, done the job, and slipped out again.'

Bates was doubtful. 'It would've been a hell of a risk, sir. Any of the staff could have seen him.'

'I agree — but they didn't.'

'There's another snag, sir — and a hefty one. How would he know *which* cubicle Mrs. Radford was in? They don't always put people in the same one.'

Merritt frowned. 'H'm! You've got something there.'

'I'd sooner go for Gabriel or Sara Graham. They had a better opportunity . . .'

'Yes,' Merritt assented. 'However, there might have been somebody in the salon that afternoon who had a better motive

259

than any of the ones we know . . .

'Look, Bates, be a good chap and rustle up a couple of cups of tea, will you? I can think better on tea — even if it is canteen dishwater!'

Bates grinned. 'Right you are, sir.'

After the sergeant had left, Merritt pondered the case as he sat at his desk. Abruptly, his expression changed.

'I wonder . . . ' he murmured under his breath. He reached for the telephone and lifted the receiver.

'Get me extension sixteen, please . . . Hello. Is Superintendent Harris there . . . ? That you, Charlie . . . ? Bill here. If you can summon up enough energy to move, perhaps you'd pop into my office? I'd like to have a little chat . . . Yes, I think you might be able to give me some information . . . '

★ ★ ★

Sara Graham and Monty Beresford were seated together in the corner of a teashop. Sara lowered her cup as she regarded Beresford with disfavour.

'I've met a few absolute lunatics in my life, but you're the biggest I've ever come in contact with!'

'Thanks!'

'Why did you have to sign a cheque with Marian's name? You must have known it would be discovered . . . '

Beresford played absently with his teaspoon. 'It was only because it had Marian's name on it that Jacobson cashed it.'

'But it was a *forgery*, Monty!'

'I was going to get the money from Marian to take up the cheque before there was any trouble.'

'Did she know about the cheque?'

Beresford looked up sheepishly. 'Well . . . no, not exactly . . . '

'She'd never have stood for that, and you know it! What are you going to do?'

Beresford considered. 'I might get an advance from old Withersfield . . . '

Sara shook her head. 'You'd better not do that . . . Look here, *I'll* lend you the money . . . '

Beresford's face lightened at this unexpected largesse. 'That's damned good of you, old girl!'

'I'm not giving it to *you*. I'll see Jacobson and fix it. I know him. He won't fool about with me.'

'I don't know why you should do this for me, Sara . . . '

'I don't, either! You're quite hopeless, Monty.'

Beresford gave a self-pitying smile. 'I know. I'm always making up my mind to stop being a fool, but it doesn't last. Something always goes wrong.'

'The thing that goes wrong, Monty, is *you*!' Sara said impatiently. 'What are you going to do when you get the money Marian left you?'

'I don't know — pay a few debts . . . '

'And drink the rest, I suppose?

'Oh, come now, that's a bit unkind! I thought of clearing off to somewhere . . . '

Sara smiled cynically. 'What makes you think you'd be any less of a weakling in another part of the world?'

Beresford winced. 'You don't mince your words, do you?'

'No, I don't . . . Now, listen to me. Why don't you pull yourself together? Stop soaking up whisky like a sponge and become a decent member of society . . . '

'Bit too late for that . . . '

'Rubbish!' Sara snapped scornfully. 'Snap out it, Monty! Get yourself a job — any job — and stick to it. There must be *something* you can do . . . '

'Precious little anyone'd pay me for!'

'I don't believe that. I think in spite of all your faults there's a bit of good in you somewhere, Monty. Dig it up.'

'I've made *so* many resolutions, Sara . . . ' Beresford said ruefully.

'Well make another — and keep it, this time.' Sara reached for her handbag and stood up. 'Now, I must be off! I've said all I've got to say. I shan't say it again. Bye-bye!'

* * *

It was late afternoon and the daylight was fading. Merritt was working at his desk under the office lights. He glanced up as a big, jovial-looking man entered.

Chief Superintendent Harris was carrying a C.R.O. file. 'Well, I've got what you wanted,' he announced, holding up the file.

'That's very good of you, Charlie. That it?'

Harris nodded and placed the file on Merritt's desk. 'I'm naturally kind-hearted! I *was* going home early this evening. I like to see my family once in a while!'

'They'll appreciate you all the more when you *do* get home.'

'You don't know my family . . . ' Harris smiled crookedly. 'Here's the dope. It's a bit meagre. It happened just outside Manchester in July of nineteen fifty-nine. A girl named Mavis Edwards found a middle-aged woman on a park seat. The woman, a Mrs. Darnley, was dead . . . '

'From an injection of cobra venom?'

'That's right. There was a mark on the side of her neck.'

Merritt's eyes gleamed. 'Like Mrs. Radford.'

'Exactly. And if it's going to cheer you up, the killer was never found!'

'Any motive?'

'There was a good bit of money

involved, apparently, which went to the husband,' Harris answered, 'but he'd been in Manchester all day on business.'

'Anybody else with a motive?'

'There was a nephew who inherited something, but the police were satisfied that he had nothing to do with it.'

'What about the girl?'

'Edwards? She was a stranger. Didn't know Mrs. Darnley or the husband. Didn't even live in the district . . . '

Merritt continued to ask questions as he began sorting through the file.

'What was she doing there — in this park?'

Harris shrugged. 'Doesn't say in the record. I expect the Manchester C.I.D. would have more details.'

Merritt glanced up from the file. 'You've got a photograph of the dead woman and a photograph of the husband here, but none of the girl.'

'They didn't include one. Thought she wasn't important enough, I suppose. Well, there you are. I'm off home.' Harris glanced at his watch and turned to take his leave. 'Let me have the file back as soon as you've finished with it.'

'All right, Charlie — and thanks a lot.'

Harris paused at the door. 'Don't mention it. If I'm hauled up in the divorce court, it'll be your fault!'

As Harris opened the door, Bates stepped into the office.

'Oh, good evening, sir,' Bates greeted Harris, who merely grunted as he exited.

'He's in a bit of a hurry, isn't he, sir?' Bates remarked.

'Anxious to get home to his family.'

Bates smiled. 'That's quite a good idea . . . '

'Maybe.' Merritt looked up as he closed the folder with a snap. 'But you can forget it. I've got a job for you.'

'Oh!' Bates looked crestfallen.

'See this file?' Merritt handed the file to Bates, who took it automatically. 'It contains the report of a murder near Manchester in nineteen fifty-nine. I want you to go to Manchester and get hold of all the details you can.

'When do I go, sir?' Bates accepted the assignment phlegmatically.

Merritt got up from his desk, and went

over to the hat-stand. He turned as he shrugged himself into his coat.

'You can catch the next train. You can read all that's in that file on the way. I want everything the Manchester police can tell you — statements, photographs, *everything*.'

'Right you are, sir.'

'Get back as soon as you can — and don't bash the expense account!'

'How does this tie up with the Radford business, sir?' Bates asked, puzzled.

'You'll see when you've read those reports.' Merritt headed for the door.

'What are you going to do, sir?'

Merritt yawned. 'I'm going home to bed!'

★　★　★

In the teeming street outside a West End Tube station, June Carter and Susann Ingram were deep in conversation as they moved with the throng. Both were dressed in street clothing, and Susann was carrying an umbrella.

'If I have another day like this, I'll be a

'nervous wreck!' Jean was exclaiming.

'It *was* hectic!' Susann agreed.

'Hectic? That blasted phone never stopped! I shall hear it in my sleep. What with that and Gabriel prancing about like an egg-bound hen, I feel all-in!'

Susann glanced at her watch. 'We're an hour later than usual.'

'Yes. I don't know what my boyfriend's going to say. Picking me up for a dance, he was. Perhaps he'll wait . . . '

'I'm going straight to bed,' Susann said. 'My feet are killing me.'

'We ought to have taken a taxi and charged it to old Gabriel! He'd probably rush for his smelling salts!'

Susann smiled. 'He's pretty jittery, isn't he?'

'Sometimes he's practically gaga! Well, here's your Tube station, dear — and there's my bus. Goodnight.'

'Goodnight, Jean.'

The receptionist hurried off, and Susann turned into the Tube station entrance. She fed money into one of the ticket machines, and then passed to the turnstiles, where she inserted and collected her ticket again before descending the escalator.

She passed along the passage leading to her platform, where she waited for her train, uncomfortable in the jostling crowd. The jostling grew worse at the sounds of an approaching train, as people moved to the edge of the platform to get ready to dart aboard the incoming carriages and try to secure a seat.

Susann felt a sudden pressure in her back, and an expression of surprise and fear flashed across her face.

The sound of a woman's sudden and shrill agonized scream sounded above the noise of the incoming train, then cut out abruptly.

There were confused cries and shouts of alarm . . .

4

In the *Maison Gabriel*, its proprietor stood by the reception desk, talking on the telephone. It was still fairly early in the morning, and his staff had not yet arrived.

There was an expression of profound shock on his face.

'But how dreadful! No, no, please don't tell me any of the details — I'm terribly sensitive to such things. I shall feel quite ill the rest of the day . . . Yes . . . Thank you for ringing me.'

As he replaced the receiver with a trembling hand, Jane Carter entered the salon. She was flushed from hurrying.

'I'm sorry I'm a little late, Mr. Gabriel,' she apologised breathlessly. 'That wretched bus — ' She broke off, regarding her employer quizzically. 'What's the matter? Are you ill?'

'I've just had the most appalling news, Jean. Susann is dead . . . '

'*Dead?*'

'She fell in front of a Tube train last night . . . '

'Oh, no!' Jean's expression was one of shock.

'It's made me feel quite faint,' Gabriel mumbled.

'Where — where did it happen?' Jean had divested herself of her coat, and was now wearing her uniform. She slipped into her seat at the reception desk.

'At the Tube station — just round the corner . . . Oh, dear!' Gabriel's voice wavered as a sudden thought struck him. 'We shall never get through the day with one assistant short . . . '

Jean shook her head dazedly. 'I can't believe it. I — I left her at the station last night . . . '

Gabriel jerked his right hand in a semi-circle, as if waving the subject away. 'I don't want to talk about it. It upsets me . . . Get on to the agency, see if they can send a girl. Tell them she must be thoroughly experienced . . . ' He glanced at his watch. 'We open in ten minutes and my nerves are absolutely shattered! I must go and find my smelling salts . . . '

Jean glared at his departing back as he headed for his office. 'Selfish old brute!' she muttered under her breath as she picked up the telephone.

★ ★ ★

In Superintendent Merritt's office at Scotland Yard, the toxicology expert was sitting by his desk, smiling complacently whilst Merritt scanned his report.

Merritt looked up at Smithson, frowning slightly. 'Are you telling me that *all* these places have cobra venom?'

'Surprised me, too,' Smithson admitted. 'Of course, there are a number of zoos included — where they've got a reptile house.'

'Why zoos?'

'They extract the venom.' As Merritt nodded, Smithson added: 'It'll keep you amused for quite a time sorting that lot out. There might even be one or two more to come.'

'Thanks.' Merritt laid the report aside. 'We'll check up and see if any of the people on our list could have connections with any of these places . . . I must say, you've been quick.'

Smithson smiled. 'Organisation, old man! Can I do anything else for you?'

'Not for the moment. If there's . . . ' Merritt broke off as his telephone rang, and picked up the receiver.

'Merritt here . . . ' He assumed a startled expression as he listened to his caller. 'Who . . . ? Oh, I see.' He glanced significantly at Smithson. 'When was this . . . ? I see . . . Was the platform crowded? H'm . . . Anybody see her fall . . . ? I see . . . Well, of course, she wouldn't have stood a chance, would she? Yes, I quite agree . . . Thanks.'

As Merritt replaced the receiver, he looked at Smithson expressively. 'Well, that's one for the books!'

'What is?'

'Susann Ingram — the girl who found Mrs. Radford — was killed last night. She fell under a Tube train.'

Smithson straightened in his seat. 'That's a pretty nasty way to die. Accident?'

'I suppose so. She fell on the live rail . . . '

'Electrocuted, eh?'

Merritt nodded. 'As well as being smashed up by the train . . . ' He broke off, frowning at a sudden thought. 'H'm, I wonder . . . ?'

'Something biting you?'

'I'd like to know more about that girl's death.'

'Are you suggesting that it *wasn't* an accident?'

'I don't know,' Merritt said slowly. 'If she'd seen something or heard something that afternoon when Mrs. Radford was murdered, her death might be very convenient for somebody . . . '

★　★　★

Lounging in an armchair, Adrian Radford was listening to music whilst reading a magazine. He looked up at the faint sounds of front-door chimes and the door being opened. There was a murmur of voices, and then the door to his room was opened and his manservant, Chub, appeared in the doorway.

'Miss Graham, sir.'

As Sara entered, Chub exited discreetly.

Adrian rose to greet her. 'Sara! How nice of you to come and cheer me up.'

'I haven't!' Sara said briefly, her expression troubled. She dropped wearily on to the settee as Adrian moved to a side-table.

'What'll you have — brandy?'

'Nothing for me, thanks.'

Adrian turned in surprise. 'What's the matter? Aren't you well?'

Sara looked at him. 'Haven't you seen the papers?'

Adrian shrugged carelessly. 'No — they're always so depressing. Is there something I should have seen?'

'That girl, Susann, fell under a train last night and was killed.'

'Susann?' Adrian spoke absently, pouring himself a drink.

'The girl at *Maison Gabriel*. I've only just heard about it. I've been out of town all day . . . '

Adrian turned back towards Sara, drink in hand. 'You mean the girl who used to attend to — to poor Marian?

'Yes. Isn't it dreadful?'

Adrian nodded. 'Nasty thing to have

happened.' He joined Sara on the settee. 'Why are you so upset about this girl? Did you know her well?'

'I scarcely knew her at all. I've spoken to her once or twice at *Maison Gabriel*, of course . . . '

Adrian took a quick drink. 'It's a ghastly thing to have happened, but I don't see why it should affect you so badly.'

'I suppose it was coming on top of Marian's death. Because she worked in the same place . . . '

Adrian's normally bland expression became clouded over. 'I can't get over that — Marian, I mean. It's like a nightmare. You've no idea what this place is like without her.' Abruptly, he stood up, and began to pace about the room. 'I can't stick it — everything reminds me of her . . . As soon as the — the funeral's over, I shall clear off!'

Sara looked at him sharply. 'Where to?

'Oh, I don't know — anywhere. Tangier, for a start, probably . . . Have you heard anything from the police?'

Sara shook her head. 'I suppose they're

doing *something*, but there hasn't been a lot of time . . . '

Adrian resumed his pacing. 'Who could have done it, Sara? Marian was so . . . sweet. She lent that pansy hairdresser seven thousand pounds . . . '

'Yes, I know.'

'She was always helping people. That waster Beresford was always running to her to get him out of some scrape or other . . . '

'He won't be able to anymore,' Sara said quietly.

'I hope he doesn't try it on with me.' Adrian's tone was belligerent. 'He'll get a few home truths if he does.

'I don't think you need worry about that, Adrian.'

Adrian stopped pacing and gave her a quizzical look. 'You've always had a soft spot for him, haven't you? Can't understand why . . . '

Sara smiled wryly. 'Monty's never fully grown up. Marian understood him . . . '

'Well enough to divorce him?' Adrian said bitingly. Then he shrugged. 'Oh well, what does it matter now? What does anything matter?'

Sara frowned. 'Except to find out who killed Marian. That matters, surely?'

Adrian turned away. 'That won't bring her back, Sara. Nothing can bring her back.'

★   ★   ★

Sergeant Bates was relaxing luxuriously in Merritt's chair. He looked distinctly travel-stained and weary. Faintly through the window came the sound of Big Ben striking four.

Suddenly the door opened and Merritt entered his office. He gave Bates a critical glance. 'Hello, Bates. When did you get back?'

Bates jumped hastily to his feet. 'About half an hour ago, sir. I popped in for a snack and a cup of tea on the way back from the station.'

Merritt hung up his hat and coat. Turning, he said caustically: 'Sure you wouldn't like to pop up to the rest room for a nap as well?'

'No, sir. I had that on the train . . . I mean . . . that is . . . '

Abashed, Bates moved hastily aside to

allow his superior to reoccupy his desk seat. 'Well, how did you get on in Manchester?'

Bates permitted himself a wide smile. 'Pretty well, sir. I've got a surprise for you!'

'I've got one for *you*.'

Bates blinked. 'What's that, sir?'

'We'll have yours first. What have you got?

'Take a look at this, sir.' Bates reached for a photograph from his inside pocket and handed it to Merritt. 'That's a photograph of Mavis Edwards, the girl who found the body of Mrs. Darnley on the park bench. It was taken by a newspaper photographer at the inquest . . . '

Merritt studied the photograph interestedly. 'H'm . . . For 'Mavis Edwards', substitute 'Susann Ingram', eh?'

'There's not much doubt, is there, sir? Hair's done differently, but you can't mistake her.'

'No, there's no mistake.'

Bates looked pleased with himself. 'I thought you'd be surprised . . . '

Merritt smiled faintly. 'Sorry to spoil your dramatic revelation, Bates, but I rather expected something of the sort.'

Bates looked crestfallen. 'I don't see how you could have connected this girl, Edwards, with Susann Ingram . . . '

'Things have been happening while you've been away, my lad. Susann Ingram, if that's her name — which I doubt — is dead.'

Bates gave a start. 'Dead!'

'She fell in front of a Tube train the night before last,' Merritt told him. 'What the train didn't do to her, the live rail did.'

'Suicide, sir?'

Merritt shrugged. 'Might be, but I'm sceptical.' Getting to his feet, he moved across his office to a filing cabinet. There was a lady's umbrella lying on top of it. He picked it up and came back to his desk, where he handed it to Bates.

'Look at this, will you?'

'What about it?' Bates' tone was bland. 'It's only a woman's umbrella . . . '

'Susann Ingram's umbrella — it was thrown clear of the train.'

Bates was looking at the umbrella more closely. 'Oh, yes, I remember it now. She had it with her when she left the salon — '

' — on the afternoon Mrs. Radford was killed. Exactly. Get hold of the handle, Bates, and twist it . . . '

Bates gave him a questioning look, then did as he was bidden. To his surprise, the handle unscrewed, and finally came away in his hand.

'It's hollow, sir!' Bates exclaimed.

Merritt nodded and opened the top drawer of the filing cabinet, from which he took a hypodermic syringe. 'And *this* fits snugly inside it, Bates.'

'A hypodermic, sir . . . '

'*The* hypodermic, Bates. The lab says it still contains cobra venom.'

Bates narrowed his eyes. 'So that's how she got it out of the place, sir. This means she killed Mrs. Radford.'

Merritt nodded. 'Yes. And since we've identified her as 'Mavis Edwards', it means that she also killed Mrs. Darnley on that park seat.'

He returned the hypodermic to the cabinet drawer, and took back the umbrella from Bates.

'But why?' Bates spread his hands. 'Was she a homicidal maniac?'

'There's much more to it than that,' Merritt said, returning to his desk. 'What else did you get hold of in Manchester?'

'Well, sir, I more or less got the whole set-up. This Mrs. Darnley was a fairly rich widow. Her husband made a fortune in property dealings, and left it all to her when she died. About six months before her death, she married Richard Darnley. He was much younger than she was, but apparently they were very happy.'

'And he got all the money?'

'That's right, sir. Of course, he was the first person they suspected, but he was in Manchester all that day and could prove it . . .'

'What happened to him afterwards?' Merritt asked.

'He sold the house and disappeared.'

'There was no evidence at all to connect him with 'Mavis Edwards'?'

'None, sir,' Bates answered. 'She didn't even live in the area. She was on a kind of walking tour, I believe. The police checked up on her, of course, but she seemed quite genuine.'

'She would be! I suppose you realise

that the Radford murder is almost a replica of the Darnley business?'

'I see what you're getting at, sir.'

Merritt sighed. 'It's always the same. They do it once and get away with it, and then they do it again . . . and again . . . '

'I'm getting the picture, sir. In each case, the husband had a complete alibi.'

'That's the hub of the whole plan. The husband's bound to be suspected because he has the greatest motive, so he's *got* to make it obvious that he couldn't have done it . . . '

'And in actual fact, sir, he didn't,' Bates pointed out. 'The girl does the actual killing . . . '

'Without much danger of suspicion. She doesn't benefit in any way. There's no connection at all between the killer and the victim . . . '

Bates frowned. 'But why should she do it?'

Merritt sat back in his chair. 'Oh, come now, Bates, use your brains!' he reproached. 'She gets her cut, for one thing; and for another, she's probably infatuated with the man she works with. It's more than likely they're married. She'd take that pre-caution if she were sensible . . . '

Bates remembered something important. 'I've brought back a press photograph of Darnley, sir, as well as the one that was in the file.' He leaned over the desk and sorted through the contents of the file. 'Here it is. He's not a bit like Radford.'

Merritt leaned forward and examined the photograph intently.

'Not on the surface. Darnley has a moustache, and his eyebrows are much fuller — it's surprising what difference that can make. Added to which, he's a good few stones lighter than Radford — but considering it's over five years ago . . . '

'But you've no doubt that Darnley is Radford?'

Merritt said: 'It'll take more than a couple of photographs — and not very good ones at that — to convince me that Darnley couldn't have altered his appearance if he wanted to.'

'In that case, sir, surely someone would be able to identify Radford as Darnley?

'After all this time?' Merritt shook his head. 'I doubt it. And supposing they did?

What could we do about it?'

'Mm. See what you mean, sir,' Bates said pensively. 'We've no charge against him.'

'That's the snag,' Merritt agreed. 'It may be a very strange coincidence that both his wives died from a shot of cobra venom, but there's absolutely no evidence that he had a hand in it.'

'The girl takes the rap, eh?'

'Exactly. A clever counsel would say what you've said — that she was a homicidal maniac. If we could *prove* that there was a connection between them, *then* we might get somewhere.'

'And that's not going to be easy now she's dead,' Bates said.

'He made sure of that, didn't he? Quite clever. A slight shove on a crowded platform at the right moment — and the only person who might be dangerous to him in the future is eliminated.'

'We've found a real beauty, sir,' Bates said disgustedly.

'And he's sitting pretty. I can't even get at him for the murder of the girl. There's absolutely nothing to show that it isn't an accident.'

'Or suicide.'

'Oh, they'll say it was that all right when it becomes known that he killed Mrs. Radford.'

'There must be some way we can get at him, sir. If this girl and Radford — or whatever his name is — were married, there must be some record.'

Merritt shrugged. 'In what name, and where? I hoped I might find the certificate at her flat — a woman usually hangs on to a marriage certificate like grim death. But there was nothing worth a row of beans! I went through the place with a fine-toothed comb . . . We might try checking back on Radford.'

'And the girl, sir.'

'Yes. You say she was supposed to be on a walking tour, then she — er — *found* Mrs. Darnley? She must have given an address to the police.'

'She did. It was a room in a lodging house at a place named Radnet, near Preston. She had a job in a zoo . . . '

Merritt gave him a sharp look. 'A zoo? What kind of a job did she have?'

'Something in the office, I believe . . . '

Merritt slapped the desk with his hand, his eyes gleaming. 'That's where the cobra venom came from! Well, we're getting somewhere Bates — even if it's not very far!'

★ ★ ★

'Thank you, Miss Croft. I've altered the time of your appointment . . . Goodbye.'

Jean Carter replaced her telephone receiver, and picked up the *Maison Gabriel* appointment book. Across the salon, her employer was clearly flustered, and there was a look of extreme annoyance on his face.

He glared at Sergeant Bates. 'This is persecution — positively persecution! Am I never to be left in peace?'

Bates remained imperturbable. 'I'm very sorry, sir, to have to disturb you in the middle of your work . . . '

Gabriel gesticulated. 'My work! The creation of beauty! Amid all these interruptions, how can it reach full flower?'

'Very trying for you, sir, I'm sure, but I should like you to tell me all you know concerning Susann Ingram.'

Gabriel gave him a blank look. 'My dear sir, I know nothing. Nothing at all. The private affairs of my assistants do not concern me.'

'But she must have told you *something* about herself when you engaged her,' Bates insisted. 'Or did you get her from an agency? It's most important that we find out all we can about her.'

'It's quite useless coming to me,' Gabriel insisted irritably. 'All I can tell you is that she applied here one day for a situation. She was a smart, attractive girl, and extremely efficient, so I engaged her . . . '

'Did she supply any references? Her previous employer? Anything like that . . . '

Gabriel shrugged. 'She had only just arrived in England from — I really can't remember where. One of the Commonwealth countries, I believe.'

'Then you know nothing about her prior to her employment here?' Bates asked deliberately.

'I thought I made that *quite* clear . . . Now, I really *must* go and attend to my clients. All these interruptions are so bad for me . . . '

'Thank you, sir,' Bates said resignedly. 'I won't bother you anymore.'

★ ★ ★

After Bates had finished delivering his negative report to Superintendent Merritt at Scotland Yard, his superior gave him a worried look.

'Just nothing at all that we can get our teeth into, Bates. There's no trace of Susann Ingram before she turned up at *Maison Gabriel.* And there's no trace of Mavis Edwards before she took that job at Radnet Zoo.'

Bates took a seat near Merritt's desk. 'Or afterwards, sir?'

'No. She left her job at the zoo a month after the Darnley business, and nobody seems to have heard of her since.'

'What about Radford?'

'Nothing! He appeared from somewhere out of the blue — supposedly from South Africa. But he's covered his tracks both as Darnley and as Radford. I don't suppose either is his real name.'

'There's no trace at Somerset House, sir,' Bates said.

'There's no trace anywhere! Oh, these two were fly, all right. But then, they'd got to be. They made quite a business out of murder, I mean.' Merritt sighed and glanced at the reports on his desk. 'Well, we know the Radford job wasn't the first. But Marian Radford was a *big* killing. Real money. They stuck to their original plan — the same modus operandi — but either Radford got tired of his accomplice, or he decided he'd be safer on his own. So he got rid of her.'

'Pleasant sort of a chap, sir!'

'Very! And I'm very much afraid he's going to slip through our fingers, Bates, and join the ranks of others we *know* are guilty but can't touch from lack of evidence.'

'Radford's got no alibi for the time the girl was killed, sir,' Bates pointed out hopefully.

'I know. He was out. But there's no evidence to show that he was anywhere near that Tube station. We can't even pin that on him!'

'If only someone had seen him do it,' Bates mused.

'Yes, but they didn't. Radford's as safe as houses — with all the money in the world to enjoy himself. Unless we can prove some link between him and the girl, I'm afraid we're helpless — completely helpless.'

5

Outside Adrian Radford's flat, a man approached purposefully. He thumbed the door button hard, and took a step back as the chimes sounded within.

At length, the door was opened by Chub the manservant. A flicker of surprise fled transiently across his poker face as he beheld Montague Beresford — but a Montague Beresford who was more smartly dressed than usual, and who was quite sober.

'Yes, sir?'

'Mr. Radford in?' Beresford demanded crisply.

'What name shall I tell him, sir?'

'Beresford — Montague Beresford.'

'I'll see if Mr. Radford is disengaged, sir. Will you . . . ' He broke off as Adrian's voice sounded behind him.

'Who's that, Chub?'

'A Mr. Beres- —'

'It's me, Radford — Beresford!' He pushed past Chub and into the hall. 'I want to see you.'

Chub was taken by surprise, and was unable to prevent Beresford from reaching Radford's lounge and striding in.

Adrian Radford was on his feet, and looking thunderous. 'I've nothing to say to you, Beresford! You can clear out! Chub! Where the hell are you?'

Chub entered nervously. 'I'm sorry, sir. I couldn't stop him.'

'Well, you can damn well show him out. I've nothing to say to him!'

'You'll be sorry if he does,' Beresford warned darkly. 'I won't keep you long.'

Radford hesitated, uncertain at the odd tone in Beresford's voice. 'Oh, very well. I'll give you two minutes. And that's all. Now — what do you want?'

Beresford nodded behind him. 'It's rather private . . . '

'All right, Chub, you can go,' Radford said irritably.

After the door had closed behind Chub, Radford snapped: 'Well, what is it? Only two minutes, mind.'

Beresford smiled with humour. 'That'll be enough.'

Radford moved over to a side-table and poured himself a single drink with studied insolence. He took a long swallow, and made no effort to offer refreshment to his unwelcome visitor.

'If you've come sponging . . . ' he began.

Beresford was watching him closely. 'I haven't. But you'd better keep a civil tongue in your head, Radford, or I may change my mind'

Radford frowned. 'What are you talking about?'

'I may go to the police instead.'

Radford took another quick drink from his glass.

'The police? What about?'

'That girl — Susann Ingram.'

'I don't know what you mean.' Radford scowled. 'Are you drunk?'

'Surprising as it may seem — I'm not,' Beresford said genially. 'I happened to be at a certain Tube station the other night, Radford.'

'Tube station?' Radford moistened his lips.

'It's no use pretending you don't

understand.' Beresford smiled sardoni-cally.

'I don't.' Radford essayed nonchalance as he took another drink.

Beresford took a step forward challeng-ingly. 'I'll speak more plainly, shall I? It wasn't an accident. She didn't fall in front of that train. She was pushed.'

'What's that got to do with me?' Radford said carefully.

'Everything. Because you pushed her. *I saw you do it.*'

Radford moved away from him impa-tiently. 'If you're not drunk, you're mad! Why should I want to push the girl under a train?'

'You know best about that.' Beresford smirked. 'The police would probably be very interested if I told them what I saw.'

Radford turned on him angrily. 'If this is some sort of a trick to try to get money out of me . . . '

'It isn't a trick, but I think it's worth twenty thousand pounds to keep my mouth shut.'

'I suppose you realise that's attempted blackmail?' Radford demanded.

Beresford shrugged. 'Let's just say that for a consideration I'm prepared to suffer a lapse of memory.'

'If you imagine,' Radford blustered, 'that I'm going to give you twenty thousand pounds because you've thought up some cock-and-bull story . . . '

'Please yourself. I expect Superintendent Merritt will be glad of the information. It'll give him something to think about . . . '

Radford gave a nervous laugh. 'Do you think he'd believe such a ridiculous story?'

'We'll have to see, shan't we? I don't know exactly what your connection was with the girl but if the police could prove there *was* any connection, they might start reconsidering that alibi of yours the day Marian was killed.'

'My alibi, as you call it, was cast-iron.'

Beresford nodded complacently. 'It had to be, hadn't it? It was your girlfriend who actually killed Marian . . . '

'Look here, I'm not going to listen to any more of this rubbish!' Radford snarled. 'I don't know anything about this girl. I had nothing to do with her falling in front of the train. Is that clear?'

'It would be — only I witnessed the whole thing.'

'That's a damned lie!' Radford shouted. 'You're making the whole story up to get money out of me.'

'Do I get it?'

Radford wavered. 'If you're hard up,' he said ungraciously, 'I don't mind letting you have a few hundred . . . '

'Two hundred hundreds, to be exact.'

'You can go to hell!' Radford shouted furiously.

Beresford shrugged. 'I'd sooner go to the police, thanks.' He turned as Radford watched him apprehensively. He began to open the door.

'Just a minute! Shut that door.'

Beresford closed the door obediently, and turned. 'Thought better of it?'

Radford avoided looking at him as he came back into the centre of the room. He stared absently into his glass. 'If you go spreading a lot of lies about me, it might be very inconvenient . . . It's just a farrago of rubbish, but it might start a lot of inquiries, and I'm planning to go abroad. I don't want to be held up . . . '

'I don't suppose you do,' Beresford said blandly.

'I'll write you a cheque . . . '

'Oh, no — cash!'

'Damn you,' Radford fumed, 'do you think I keep all that amount in the place?'

'Tomorrow will do. Bring it round to my flat.' Beresford turned to go.

'Who the devil do you think I am?' Radford demanded. 'Your servant?'

Beresford smiled imperturbably. 'I'll be in at seven.'

Radford lost control all of his composure. 'You blasted swine! I'd like to — '

Beresford paused, his hand on the doorknob. 'Get me on a Tube station platform — just as the train was coming in? You won't get the chance!'

He opened the door and turned, genially waving his hand. 'Don't forget — seven o'clock!'

He exited, closing the door quietly behind him. Radford stared after him for a few moments, then turned and viciously hurled his glass into the fireplace.

Sergeant Bates was standing at an open filing cabinet in Superintendent Merritt's office, sorting through its contents, when the door opened and Merritt returned.

Bates looked up. 'Well, sir? What did the A.C. have to say?'

'It was more a question of what he *didn't* say!' Merritt smiled ruefully.

Bates closed the drawer of the cabinet. 'Like that, eh?'

'Just like that — only more so. Anything come in?'

Bates pointed across the room. 'On your desk, sir. Mostly negative.'

'H'm! Well, I'm not going to wade through *this* lot. You haven't missed anything, I suppose?'

'No, unfortunately.'

Merritt gave a resigned sigh. 'Oh well, that's that!'

'We'll just have to keep our fingers crossed, sir.'

Merritt sat at his desk. 'I'm all against the third degree, but there are times when I wish we could use a bit of it.'

'I'm with you, sir. I wouldn't mind having a go at Radford myself.'

'A cool, callous devil. And we can't even ask him a single question that might incriminate him. It makes me see red!'

'Cheer up, sir.'

Merritt gave him a sour look. 'You didn't have to face the A.C. this morning. If this thing goes wrong, it *could* result in my resignation, you know!'

★ ★ ★

In Monty Beresford's flat a small clock in his lounge was striking seven.

Beresford had just poured himself a drink. He held it up to the light, then drank the contents appreciatively. He smiled quietly to himself as there sounded a peremptory knocking on his front door.

Putting down his glass, he passed through the open door into the small hall and opened his front door.

Adrian Radford was standing outside, wearing hat, coat, and gloves. In his left hand he was carrying a bulky briefcase.

'Punctual to the minute,' Beresford

observed pleasantly. 'Come in.'

Sour-faced, Radford entered without speaking and passed through into the lounge. Beresford closed the front door and came in behind him.

'I see that briefcase bulging pleasantly,' he remarked.

Radford turned. 'Let's get the thing done with. I don't want to hang about here longer than necessary.' His voice was bitter and resentful.

Beresford shrugged. 'All right. Dump the money on the table.'

Radford put his briefcase on the table and snapped back the catch. 'I'm not leaving the briefcase.'

So saying, he tipped the contents of the case onto the table — bundles of banknotes. 'There's your pound of flesh, blast you!'

Beresford eyed the money speculatively. 'You won't miss it — out of all the money Marian left you.'

'You're not doing so badly, are you, Beresford?' Radford sneered. 'Five thousand from Marian, and twenty thousand from blackmail!'

'I prefer to call it, 'for services rendered'.'

Radford closed the briefcase. 'Whatever you call it, it's the same thing! I've got to trust you not to go spreading those damned lies about me, I suppose?'

Beresford smiled derisively. 'Lies? You don't pay twenty thousand pounds to stop somebody telling lies, Radford!

'I've told you, I don't want any trouble . . . '

'Naturally. Your association with the dead girl might come out. And then you'd *really* be in the soup!'

'I tell you, there *was* no association!' Radford said angrily.

'You killed her for fun, I suppose? Don't try to bluff it out with me, Beresford. I was an eyewitness — remember?'

Radford scowled. 'What were you doing at that Tube station, anyway?'

'Does that matter?' Beresford shrugged. 'I saw you — and that's what counts.'

'I don't believe you. I should have seen — ' Radford stopped abruptly as he realised his words were incriminating.

'Go on — finish it! 'I should have seen you' is what you were going to say, isn't it?'

Radford glared at his tormentor. 'You damned, lousy spy . . . '

'Why lose your temper?' Beresford said evenly. 'I shan't give you away. That'd be killing the golden goose, wouldn't it?'

'If you think you're going to bleed me of any more . . . '

Beresford chuckled. 'Don't worry. I shan't — unless I get hard up, of course!'

'You blasted swine!' Radford was choking with fury.

'Oh, come now,' Beresford chided. 'What's the use of slanging me? We might as well be civilised about this. Let's have a drink, and seal the bargain.' He sauntered over to the side table and uncorked a bottle.

Radford watched him narrowly. 'You're a pretty cool customer, aren't you, Beresford?'

Beresford nodded complacently. 'I believe in looking after myself.' He proceeded to pour out a couple of drinks, and offered one to Radford.

'Here you are — a nice stiff Scotch. It'll do you good.' He raised his glass in a taunting toast. 'Here's to our little deal . . . '

Radford raised his own glass with reluctant distaste, then suddenly stiffened.

'*Listen!*' he exclaimed.

'What's the matter?' Beresford wrinkled his brow.

'I thought I heard someone in your hall . . . '

Beresford frowned. 'I didn't hear anything.'

'Are you sure you shut the front door?' Radford demanded. Then, accusingly: 'If this is one of your little games . . . '

'Don't be silly. Why should it be?' Beresford put down his glass. 'I'll go and have a look, all the same . . . '

As Beresford exited into the hall, Radford moved to the side table and put down his own glass. He cast a swift glance in the direction of the doorway: there was no one there. His gloved hand took something from his pocket, and then quickly passed it over Beresford's glass.

'Nothing here.' Beresford's voice sounded from the hall. 'You must have imagined it.'

Seconds later, Beresford re-entered, smiling broadly. He found Radford in his original position, glumly fingering his own glass.

'You ought to take a grip of yourself, old boy!' Beresford looked about him. 'Where's my drink? Oh, here.'

He retrieved his glass from the table, raised it again in a mock salute to Radford, and then lifted it to his lips.

'*Don't touch that whisky, Mr. Beresford!*' Merritt's urgent voice rang out across the room.

Radford swung round in complete astonishment. 'What the hell . . . '

He beheld the grim and purposeful figures of Merritt and Bates entering from another door in the room.

'Look after that drink, Bates,' Merritt commanded crisply. 'I don't know what he's put in it, but the lab will be able to tell us.'

Beresford looked at his glass in stupefaction, then put it down hastily. Radford began to back away, blustering. 'I don't know what the devil you mean by this . . . '

'It's no good, Radford,' Merritt told him. 'We were watching you from behind the partly open door to the kitchen. You slipped something into Mr. Beresford's drink when he went into the hall.'

'You rat, Beresford!' Radford fumed. 'You damned, lousy rat . . . '

'That'll do,' said Merritt brusquely. 'It's my duty to warn you that anything you say will be taken down, and may be used in evidence hereafter.'

'You've nothing on me . . . ' Radford began, desperation in his voice.

'I'm taking you into custody on a charge of attempting to murder Montague Beresford by poison,' Merritt said deliberately. 'There will probably be more serious charges.'

'That dirty swine was blackmailing me . . . ' Radford began wildly.

'We know all about that. Take him down to the squad car, Bates.'

Bates moved swiftly forward towards Radford. 'Yes, sir.'

'You can't . . . ' Radford began backing away. ' . . . you can't . . . '

'Come along — ' Bates grabbed him tightly by an arm.

Radford struggled furiously. 'I won't

. . . Get your hands off me — '

Bates got a firm judo hold on Radford and twisted his arm behind his back.

'You'll get hurt if you try that on,' Bates told him. '*Now* will you come quietly?'

'My arm! You're breaking my arm!'

Ignoring his protests, Bates frog-marched his struggling prisoner unceremoniously towards the hall.

Beresford watched their departure dazedly until the front door slammed behind them. Then he turned towards Merritt with a shaky laugh.

'I think I need a *real* drink after that!'

'You deserve it, sir,' Merritt said. 'You put the whole bluff over very nicely.'

Beresford reached for a bottle. 'Wouldn't *you* like a drink, too?'

'Well, I wouldn't say no.' Merritt smiled. 'I don't mind telling you, I've been sweating back there in case anything went wrong. I'd probably have had to resign!'

Beresford poured out a generous measure of whisky.

'He swallowed the whole story, didn't he?' Beresford offered a glass. 'Here you are, Superintendent.'

Merritt accepted the drink. 'Thanks. It was dicey enough. If it *had* been an accident . . . Well, it came off. We can hold him now until we can sort out enough evidence to charge him with the lot.'

He sipped the whisky appreciatively.

'Did you expect he'd have a shot at getting rid of me?' Beresford asked curiously.

'I reckoned he'd try something of the sort, sir. You were a danger to him while you remained alive. He could never feel really safe . . . and murder becomes a habit.'

Beresford gave a little shudder. 'I suppose he'd have taken the money away after I was dead, and it would have been put down to suicide?'

Merritt nodded. 'That's about it, sir. Did you notice he kept his gloves on? There'd have been only your fingerprints on the glass . . . and the inference would have been obvious.'

Beresford sighed with relief. 'Well, I'm glad it's over . . . ' He paused, then added, a little bitterly, 'It's about the only really decent thing I've ever done in my life, I suppose. I'm a good liar, you know! He really *did* think I'd seen him kill that girl . . . '

He broke off at the sound of loud knocking at the front door.

Merritt put down his glass. 'That'll be Bates. I'll go, sir.'

He exited to the hall, leaving Beresford standing pensively. He listened to the sound of the front door being opened, then gave a start as a female voice sounded:

'Can I . . . ? Oh, Superintendent Merritt! What are *you* doing here?'

'There's been a little excitement . . . ' Merritt murmured.

Beresford put down his glass and called through the open doorway:

'Come in, Sara!'

Sara Graham swept into the room. 'What's happened? Oh, good heavens!' She gasped in consternation. 'Where did all that money come from? Monty, what have you been doing?'

Beresford laughed. 'It's all right, it isn't mine.'

Merritt re-entered the room. 'I'm taking it with me, Miss Graham. I can use

Radford's briefcase.'

'Adrian?' Sara looked bewildered. 'Is that money Adrian's?'

'Mr. Beresford will tell you all about it.' Merritt smiled. 'I must be off. I've got to get that whisky to the lab.' He looked at Beresford. 'Do you happen to have a clean bottle anywhere, sir?'

'There are some empty bottles in the kitchen.'

'Fine. I'll rinse one out.' Merritt picked up the untouched glass of whisky and exited into the kitchen.

Sara looked at Beresford blankly. 'Look here, what is this all about . . . ?'

Before he could answer, there was another knock at the front door. 'Excuse me . . . ' Beresford hurried off to answer the front door, where he admitted Sergeant Bates.

Bates stepped into the lounge. 'Where's the super . . . ? Oh, good evening, Miss.'

Sara screwed up her face in exasperation. 'I wish somebody would tell me . . . '

Merritt re-entered from the kitchen, corking up a small bottle. He nodded to Bates. 'Get Radford to the car all right?'

'Yes, sir. Hobbs and Gordon are look-ing after him. He's practically foaming at the mouth.'

Merritt smiled grimly. 'That type always crack up when they find they're not as clever as they thought they were . . . Shove all that money in the briefcase, Bates, and we'll get going. Thanks for your help, Mr. Beresford.'

As Bates began filling the briefcase, Sara burst out:

'If somebody doesn't tell me what all this is about, I'll scream!'

We do hope that you have enjoyed reading this large print book.

Did you know that all of our titles are available for purchase?

We publish a wide range of high quality large print books including:
Romances, Mysteries, Classics
General Fiction
Non Fiction and Westerns

Special interest titles available in large print are:
The Little Oxford Dictionary
Music Book, Song Book
Hymn Book, Service Book

Also available from us courtesy of Oxford University Press:
Young Readers' Dictionary
(large print edition)
Young Readers' Thesaurus
(large print edition)

For further information or a free brochure, please contact us at:
Ulverscroft Large Print Books Ltd.,
The Green, Bradgate Road, Anstey,
Leicester, LE7 7FU, England.
Tel: (00 44) **0116 236 4325**
Fax: (00 44) **0116 234 0205**

SHERLOCK HOLMES: THE FOUR-HANDED GAME

Paul D. Gilbert

Holmes and Watson find themselves bombarded with an avalanche of dramatic cases! Holmes enrols Inspectors Lestrade and Bradstreet to help him play a dangerous four-handed game against an organization whose power and influence seems to know no bounds. As dissimilar as the cases seem to be — robbery, assault, and gruesome murder — Holmes suspects that each one has been meticulously designed to lure him towards a conclusion that even he could not have anticipated. However, when his brother Mycroft goes missing, he realises that he is running out of time . . .

THE MANUSCRIPT KILLER

Noel Lee

When Detective Inspector Drizzle receives a mysterious message from elderly recluse Matthew Trevelyn imploring him to visit the next day, as he is in fear of his life, Drizzle sets out straight away. Delayed by a punctured tyre, however, he arrives at the country house to discover he's too late: Trevelyn has been brutally murdered — strangled by a silk scarf belonging to his niece. Her boyfriend had been thrown out the previous night after a raging quarrel with Trevelyn — but is he the true culprit? Thus begins Drizzle's strangest case . . .